SHATTERED VISION

FRENCH · EXPRESSIONS
HOLMES & MEIER

SHATTERED VISION

RABAH BELAMRI

Translated from the French
by Hugh A. Harter

HOLMES & MEIER
New York / London

Published in the United States of America 1995 by
Holmes & Meier Publishers, Inc.
160 Broadway
New York, NY 10038

Originally published in French as *Regard blessé*, copyright © Éditions Gallimard,
Paris, 1987.

Book design by Sara Burris.

This book has been printed on acid-free paper.

Library of Congress Cataloging-in-Publication Data

Belamri, Rabah, 1946-
    [Regard blesse. English]
    Shattered vision / Rabah Belamri : translated by Hugh A. Harter.
        p.   cm. -- (French expressions)
    ISBN 0-8419-1258-0
    1. Algeria---History--Revolution, 1954-1962--Fiction 2. Teenage boys---
Algeria---Fiction. I. Harter, Hugh A.   II. Title   III. Series.PQ3989.2.B36R413
1995   94--16236
843--dc20   CIP

Manufactured in the United States of America

To Yvonne

"In the distance we can
see a transparent fire."

Jean Sénac
The Limpid Prisoner

I

March 12, 1962

A wet road gripped by winter, heights rising above it still capped with snow. The taxi slowly moves ahead. The driver who, like all Algerians, has learned to be cautious in seven years of war, keeps what he hopes is a safe distance between his vehicle and the half-track that brings up the rear of the convoy. The passengers, swaying slightly in rhythm with the curves, sit in silence. Suddenly, as though oblivious to the presence of the convoy and the gleaming death's finger of the half-track's machine gun pointed unswervingly at the taxi, they begin to talk. They talk about everything except war and their anguish. Hassan is curled up on the back seat in between his brother, who is wearing civilian clothes, and a corpulent gentleman smelling of musk.

It was on that same road in springtime, at the very beginning of the war. That day Hassan was wearing the green shirt his father had bought him the day before. He had put some bril-

9

liantine stolen from his elder brother on his hair. Aziz, a scowl on his face, was waiting in front of the blue-gray bus. He envied Hassan for leaving for Sétif without him, for getting to see the tall-storied houses all by himself, the streets, the cars, numerous stores, and the fountain with four cannons surmounted by a stone figure of a woman people said was nude. Aziz did not unclench his teeth and, trembling with frustration as the bus started up, he shook his fist at his cousin who smiled at him from behind the window. The morning sun, hot and sparkling, struck the boy squarely on the face. He opened his eyes wide to take in the full immensity of the earth that rushed by at his sides. He felt happy and at peace when all of a sudden, as it came around a curve just where the road rises a bit between a ravine and a ridge covered with bushes, the bus came to a stop. Silence and amazement: on the road, a group of men armed with hunting rifles. One of them, face masked by black glasses, came up to the driver. A few words and a commanding wave of his arm. The passengers got out, obedient and uneasy. Two men came up to look them over one after the other. The younger of the two, Hassan saw, carried a dagger as well as a cartridge belt.

Hassan had already heard people talk about those armed men who hid during the day and came out at night to cut the throat of anybody who didn't like them or refused to feed them. He remembered the evening the *caïd* and the constable had called his father and all of their neighbors who had any kind of arms to tell them to do guard duty that night because some Resistance fighters, the *fellagas*, had been sighted in the mountains. The boy heard the mysterious name for the first time, impressing him and frightening him: *fellagas,* confederates, like the *djinns,* accomplices of the night, of mountain paths, of high grass, of deep ravines, and of the stars. A few days later, he heard the name again. His father and the neighbors, submissive in their distress, turned in their rifles and their cartridges to the gendarmes. "Mama, why are they turning in their rifles?" "So the *fellagas* won't take them." "Then they aren't going to hunt pheasants any more?"

The driver got back into the bus, accompanied by two men. Under their orders, he started up the engine, shifted gears, went forward, backed up, and finally drove his vehicle to the edge of a cliff. The passengers were told to push. The empty bus slowly slid forward and tipped over into the ravine as Hassan looked on amazed. The great crash at the bottom of the cliff echoed deep inside the boy as he quietly began to cry.

A giant of a man with his head shaved and carrying a huge shining goatskin over his shoulder came out of the bushes. He went rushing nimbly down the ridge and spread out the contents of the goatskin over the bus lying there on its side with its windows smashed. He set fire to a rag. The passengers were taken away. A man with an auburn mustache came over to talk with them. He was the leader. He went up to the child with the tear-stained face and patted him on the head.

"Are you crying because you can't go to Sétif? When you grow up, the whole earth will belong to you. You'll go anywhere you like."

Hassan looked at him without understanding. He felt a tremendous sense of sadness.

The armed men disappeared without a trace. The passengers, freed from a still present danger, walked quickly down the road toward the village. Several of them began to run, and others disappeared into the fields, improvising paths for themselves. Only the bus driver, a faraway look on his face, seemed barely to move ahead. Hassan, clutching his father's sleeve, was still thinking about the big city. Then an explosion shook the countryside, forcing even those who had remained calm to start running.

The taxi driver opens his window, coughs up some phlegm, sticks his head out to spit it on the road, changes his mind, and swallows with difficulty. Careful! The military convoy is still right in front of him. The soldier looking at him from the half-track might think he was aiming that spittle at him.

"What time do you take the machine?"

"Two-thirty."

"Perfect, perfect. We have plenty of time. No need to hurry."

"That's true. Why hurry? Time does not belong to us. We are in the hands of God."

"Quite so. What's the matter with your brother?"

It's the man next to Hassan, the one smelling of musk, who has asked the question. Hassan feels himself blush: indignation, suffering, despair. He can't get used to people constantly asking about his illness, insistently questioning him through his relations. And nothing distresses and discourages him so much as the commiseration following the questions, even knowing they stem from sincere feelings. Every word of pity plunges him still deeper into the depths of night.

"The doctor said, 'A little membrane in the eye is detached.'"

"He can't see anything at all?"

"Nothing but a thin shaft of light."

"How old is he?"

"Fifteen."

"What a shame! Cut down in the prime of youth! An ear of corn that grows and is struck down by fate."

"He's so young, poor boy!"

"It's true."

"It can't be easy to live in the night all the time!"

"May God bestow the light of day on him once more!"

"So you're taking him to Algiers?"

"Yes, to the main hospital."

"Yes, they say there are fine doctors at Mustafa Hospital. Say what you like, the French have know-how. An operation and there you are. Besides, you don't feel a thing. You get a shot, and they open your body. Afterward, they sew you up with a needle and thread."

"A needle and thread?"

"Yes, a needle and thread."

"God is great. What miracles and marvels has He not permitted His creatures to perform!"

"As for me, my brothers, I do not understand. The more I look at the kid, the more I ask myself: how can it be that he sees nothing? Just look, his eyes are as clear as mine. It's not possible."

All of the passengers in the taxi take part in the discussion, but no one speaks directly to Hassan, as if he'd lost his reason and his ability to speak at the same time as his sight.

. . .

Is a cure still possible? It has been almost two months since
the ear, nose, and throat specialist who acted as oculist for Sétif
wrote up a prescription for him at the Algiers hospital, one well
equipped to take care of detached retinas. But two months went
by at home, two months without any medical observation, without
any care, with his eyes relinquished to the singular manipula-
tions of ignorance. Ignorance, even when it is nourished with
good intentions, can be nothing but devastating. Hassan was not
deceived by it. He only accepted the traditional medicines so
that he would not have to listen to his mother's voice filled more
with pain than reproach: "Do you want to stay in a corner, grop-
ing along walls?" He had even consented to go with his mother
down a mule path to consult a seer living in the mountains. After
dinner the sheik, almost totally blind himself, had run his fingers
over him for a long time as he intoned benedictions for Fatim-
Zohra's satisfaction. Actually, what the sainted man wanted was
to size up closely the height of his guest and to inform himself by
the touch of both his puberty and his thinking before allowing
him to sleep on the same mat and under the same covers as his
own family, a dozen children of both sexes and every age.

Fatim-Zohra's forebodings were confirmed. Yes, it was the
djinns that struck her son in the eyes. The seer could see them
in action on his inner mirror. They belonged to the aquatic
species, the most frightening of all, it seemed. They had surprised Hassan in the water. The mother thought about the river
where, deaf to her calls, Hassan would plunge headlong mid-

14

days in summer. She thought about the hot rains when her son, still deaf to her pleas, took off his shirt and ran howling though the downpour. She thought about the strange game Hassan habitually liked to play, one that deeply frightened her. Every time the boy came near his parents' house, he would close his eyes and grope his way along, dragging his feet to identify the terrain and brushing his hands against the hedges of gardens and the facades of houses. His mother would scold him, warning him not to play at being blind: "If you keep on inviting bad luck, you'll end up with it." Hassan laughed at her fears and, to frighten her even more, would stretch out full length along the blue cement of the room while he unbuttoned his shirt.

The next morning before he let his visitors go, the sheik picked up his reed pen and blindly composed a talisman that Hassan was to wear attached to a string around his neck. For his part, his son would do his best to find a remedy for eye ailments in an old traditional book of medicine written in Arabic and whose existence for many long centuries had earned it great prestige. To fix everything in her mind, Fatim-Zohra had the seer's son repeat everything. Preparation of the sick boy: shave his head. Ingredients of the medicine: powder of tobacco and dried oleander leaves. Usage: inhalation several times per day and pouring a pail of cold water over the patient's head every morning. Description of the healing process: the glacial drenchings will drive the humors that are the source of the illness out of the center of the skull. Drained off toward the nostrils, these humors will be eliminated thanks to the sneezing that results from the inhalations.

"The cure is certain, it is written in the book," concluded the son of the sheik as he carefully replaced the volume in a leather pouch.

Fatim-Zohra, grateful and full of hope, kissed his head: the book written in Arabic says to do so.

It was the coldest part of the winter, an exceptionally severe winter, but Hassan, with remarkable docility, went on with the treatment, even though he had no illusions about its effectiveness.

Because of Fatim-Zohra's preference for a combination of treatments—cure will be that much quicker—Hassan's sight, or what was left of it, deteriorated rapidly. One day Fatim-Zohra ground up an eathenware plate in her brass mortar. She worked at it patiently until she got a very fine powder. That evening she put several pinches of this product in her son's eyes. One of the village women, moved by Fatim-Zohra's distress, had come all the way to the house to recommend that remedy to her, swearing that she had used it to treat her own eyes. Another day, following the advice of an old woman she had met at the dispensary, she mixed olive oil, alcohol, petroleum, vinegar, extract of coal tar, resin, tanbark, salt, cloves, ginger, nutmeg, thyme, henna, gunpowder, and other strange herbs and ingredients in a bowl. The result was an ointment she used to cover Hassan's bare head. Hassan went to sleep wearing his fabulous headgear, and the next morning he was virtually blind. He vehemently blamed his mother, who broke down in tears.

Fatim-Zohra didn't feel guilty of any crime against her son: many an individual, ones she knew herself or had heard about, had tried the treatments before Hassan with satisfactory results.

16

If her son's problem so strongly withstands treatment, isn't that proof that the cause is the intervention of spirits alone? Fatim-Zohra was convinced of it. She continued to visit the holy men and soothsayers. One sorceress, holding a snake between her breasts to warm it and feeding it with a little spoon in front of her deathly frightened consultants, revealed to Fatim-Zohra that her son would recover his sight when he reached the midway point of his life: at twenty if he was to live to forty, at thirty if he was to live to sixty, age fifty if he was to live a century, and so on. She also specified that Hassan had been the victim of the evil eye. Fatim-Zohra was not surprised. Hadn't her sister-in-law Zineb, with neither children nor husband and overly sensitive, led her to believe that she had something to do with her misfortune? Because, one day walking near her, Hassan had pretended not to see her, and he hadn't kissed her. She had cried. The parents had Zineb come to the house where they gave her a good dinner and covered her with kisses, begging her indulgence and her pardon. Zineb denied the accusation. She had had nothing to do with the matter and, moreover, if she had it in her power to cure the little one, she would have done so a long time ago.

Hassan was aware of the danger he was running by staying at home. But what could he do to get to Algiers? Algiers was far away, and his father, having never been outside of their province, could not take him there. And then too the news from Algiers was not good: bombs were exploding by the dozens. Consequently, Hassan had to wait for his soldier brother, recently stationed in Algiers. At the end of his leave, he would take the boy back with him.

Doing nothing was torture for Hassan who scarcely ever came home before nightfall and then did so only because of the curfew and his parents' threats. His friends rarely came to visit him. One day followed another, monotonous and interminable. Hassan sank into a sweaty torpor. He no longer got out of bed. Ramadan provided the excuse for renouncing food. It was only with a superhuman effort accompanied by nausea that he was able to swallow half of a pear or an orange. It was as though he had no desire to go on living. In actual fact, his innermost senses and his imagination were at the boiling point. He could pick up sounds either day or night with remarkable sharpness.

Snow that winter fell in such abundance that the villagers feared for their houses. The strongest ones climbed up onto the roofs, puffing noisily as they shoveled them clean. The rules for neighborliness were cynically put to shame: no one worried about tossing shovelsful of snow down into the neighbor's yard or in front of his door, just so long as one's own roof was cleared off.

"I'm telling you not to throw another flake into my yard."

"I say shit on you! I'll throw as much as I want."

"You want to bury us? You infidel!"

"Tough luck!"

"God will punish you. It won't be long before the tables turn. You'll get yours."

Fatim-Zohra was furious. Her cries and curses could be heard all over the neighborhood. Her husband, who had just come home, said nothing. He picked up a shovel and began to clean up the snow that his neighbor went right on dumping from overhead. He ended up so tired that he couldn't climb to the roof of his own house.

"The house is going to fall down on top of us!"

"If that is our destiny, then let it fall, woman!"

One neighbor, who happened to be up on his roof, reassured Fatim-Zohra and offered his help.

"May your light blaze even brighter, my son! The earth is not populated only with scoundrels."

In his bed, Hassan suffered knowing he could not help his parents. He would have liked to punish the neighbor for his insolence. Nevertheless, he worked out a plan of vengeance that was terrible and bloody. That evening Fatim-Zohra talked about the times that weren't going to be long in coming. The war could not last more than seven years: various signs seen by proper people in their sleep made the end something to hope for. Hassan himself was aware of how their neighbor had acted the day of the great demonstration. While the enthusiastic crowd of men, women and children ran for the first time through the streets with the Algerian flag held high and waving green scarves, the man next door had hung two large French flags in his windows, where all could see them.

Night has fallen on the village. The air is brisk, and the sky is sparkling. Three men muffled up in heavy *kachabias* of brown wool approach the houses. One of them looks surprisingly like Hassan. They stoop down behind a garden hedge, ears cocked toward the path leading to the road. Soon they hear unsteady footsteps on the pebbles. Two silhouettes appear, one holding up the other.

"By God in heaven, what a lot of stones on this earth!"

The voice was that of a drunken man.

"Shut up! People will hear you. You shouldn't have gotten yourself drunk!"

"Bastard! You're the one who made me drink."

"Shut up and keep moving or I'm going to leave you right here. You can get home on your own."

"All right, all right."

The three members of the Resistance, the *maquisards*, step onto the path. Two of them try to grab hold of the drunken man, but when he suddenly sees the trap he's walked into, he begins to struggle with all his might and bites the arms and shoulders of his assailants, moaning furiously the whole time. The man who was walking with him grabs him from behind, choking him by the throat with both hands. The traitor hiccoughs, sways, and then falls half senseless on his side. The others turn him over on his back, and the youngest *maquisard*, the one who looks like Hassan, plunges his dagger three times into the man's chest. The four men quickly disappear: the soldier goes to his home nearby, and the Resistance fighters are soon lost in the night.

That, people said in low voices, was how the Arab secretary to the mayor came to his death one winter's night. The *maquisards* had warned him to withdraw from the list of candidates drawn up by the French.

"It won't be those sons of beggars and shepherds that will

make me change my mind," he'd said.

After waiting up for him all night, his wife came out at dawn. She wanted to go to the end of the pebble path to look down the road. She stumbled over the body and recognized her husband right away. Thinking he was asleep after another night of too much drinking with his friends, she tried to awaken him. She called him and shook him and and ran her hands over him until her fingers slipped on the chest sticky with blood where the knife had struck.

The village had been awakened by the cries of the woman. Hassan had trouble swallowing his breakfast. On the way to the Koranic school, he ran into Abla, the neighbors' daughter. They stopped under a tree to listen to the lamentations: "My children, my children, now you are orphans!" They went to the mosque in silence.

Gamra was beautiful. Her scent, the softness of her voice, the contact with her warm lips, slightly humid, excited her cousin. His sex swelled up. His hand grabbed it under the covers. Hassan had felt desire for his cousin for a long time. As a child he would search out where she lived, and when she spent the night at their house, he would snuggle up against her breast, his breath cut short and his heart pounding with emotion. She would take his hand and guide it between her burning thighs.

Hassan had not seen his cousin for a number of years, because the two families had stopped seeing each other for reasons never really clear. Gamra's marriage to a *harki*, an

Algerian in the Frenchmen's army, made the break even greater. Once the *harki* had disappeared, Hassan's illness became the pretext for the two families to take up the relationship once again. Seated in front of the fireplace, she talked all afternoon long. Sometimes she would burst into tears. Fatim-Zohra consoled her by reminding her that all misfortune and suffering comes to an end.

"He beat me, Auntie. He put the barrel of his rifle on my heart, shouting blasphemies: 'Yell "Vive de Gaulle" and "Death to the *fellagas* and the Arabs" or I'll blast you.' I would cry so, my eyes were like a fountain. In my heart, I cursed those who had set up my marriage. . . . 'Listen, you scum, if you aren't pregnant in three months, I'll put three bullets in your belly.' 'It's God who decides, I have nothing to do with it. If you want to take another wife, go ahead. I grant you a thousand pardons.' 'No! I want you to give me a child, and not just a child—a boy! If you have a girl, I'll cut both your throats. I swear it on the head of my mother and General de Gaulle's.' I would cry so, my eyes were like a fountain. I prayed to God to put a bullet between his eyes. The day they brought him home on a stretcher with a hole in his forehead, I didn't shed a single tear. But today who will have me? Who wants the widow of a *harki*? I'm marked for life, my youth wasted. And everybody says the war will soon be over. . . ."

So that Hassan and Gamra would not be side by side under the woolen blankets that covered the common sleeping mat, Fatim-Zohra put little Malik, her youngest boy, between them. Hassan had trouble controlling his desires. His temples were throbbing. As soon as the lamp was put out by his father, who was sleeping at the far end of the mat, his hand edged over. Malik was sound asleep. Hassan's fingers touched her gown, grazing against it and, trying to find its shape, moving about nimbly. The heavy covers did not move. The cousin was asleep or was pretending to be asleep. Hassan could make out her breathing which was quiet and regular. Gamra was lying curled up, her face turned to the other side. The hand, almost ethereal, slipped under the gown. Hassan could no longer control his breathing. The house began to resound with the crazy beating of his heart. Gamra lay still, maintaining, it seemed, regular breathing. Hassan's fingers caressed her buttocks, and then her thighs which he forced open enough to give him passage. Hassan's sex was hurting him. His body was quivering. He felt silky hair and hot, humid flesh that seemed to open up by itself. His middle finger hesitated and then slipped into the channel. Gamra's body stiffened. A hand seized Hassan's hand and squeezed it violently. Gamra turned over. Her hand found the swollen member, took hold of it, caressed it, and held it tightly. A shower of stars illuminated the fabled night. The sky turned green and split open in the center. Three *houris*, naked and aflame, appeared. They danced on Hassan's desire till dawn. At noon, Gamra went away, after having left a kiss of tenderness on her cousin's forehead.

January 1962

The chief, wrapped in a brown burnoose, is seated on an old packing box. He is thinking. His four companions, squatting in front of him, are warming their hands over a brazier. The chief begins to speak:

"We've got to move a bit. The colonel that smokes the long pipe is going to think we've definitely been wiped out."

"But who?"

"It's not targets we're short on."

"Yes, that's true. All we have to do is poke around in the heap: the recruits, the traitors, the ones who don't pay their dues, the French. . . ."

"The ideal would be to blast that bastard Thibaud. What a helluva lot of electricity he shot into me!"

"Thibaud. . . . That's not easy. As for me, I've watched him walking around the village with the butt of his revolver stuck to his thigh. And his eyes glancing from left to right."

"At any rate, it's the French we've got to hit. We've got to create a maximum of fear in them. Sparrow, you'll do the job, You aren't under suspicion. You can move around the village without any problem."

"Well then, who?"

"You'll decide on the spot. It's up to you."

The church tower clock strikes six as Sparrow walks past the *harkis'* barracks. It is cold. The main street with its leafless ash trees is deserted and silent. The merchants are inside their shops, and men of leisure in the warmth of cafés with closed doors. Sparrow strolls along nonchalantly, his hands in the pockets of his old gray overcoat. He still doesn't know what man he's going to shoot. Nevertheless, he's made his decision: he will open fire on the first Frenchman that chance puts in his path. He will scour every street of the village, if need be. He will, however, avoid going near the police station or the dragoons' barracks. "We have already carried out quite a few attacks; the colonist and the constable, the grenades thrown into cafés, the time bombs in front of food stores, harvests and vehicles set on fire. . . . But the chief said, 'We've got to create a maximum of fear in them.'"

A man dressed like a Frenchman comes up the street. He is still too far away for Sparrow to distinguish his features. He is not walking very fast. He looks big and slightly stooped. Sparrow doesn't take long to recognize in him an employee of the hospital, the eldest of the Zitoun brothers. He speaks Arabic; he's a Jew. All the same, he's French; his name is André. Sparrow has not received any special orders. He's supposed to shoot a Frenchman, period, and that's all. He comes up to the man, avoids looking at him, turns around and fires two shots. André Zitoun starts to run and calls out to his helper whose butcher shop is close by. A few yards away, he falls in the gutter. That same day, he dies in the Sétif hospital.

"So why did they kill that man? He was courteous, and had a voice as soft as honey." People asked questions in low tones. "He made contributions of money, and he closed his eyes when medicines disappeared from the hospital. But if the brothers decided on this action, they must have their reasons." Hassan knew the Monsieur André who frequented his father's grocery store and lingered to take part in the pleasant conversations with the merchant and his customers. One day he had asked Hassan to carry his shopping bags home for him. He had given him four *douros*. Hassan, who would have liked to see the inside of a Frenchman's house, didn't have the courage to cross the threshold. He left the basket in front of the door and hurried away.

After every attack, the villagers were afraid. Those who feared they were suspects avoided going out in public for a few days. There was no investigation and no arrest. People were surprised; the colonel with the long pipe wasn't a man to let a terrorist act go unpunished. People still remembered the first attack that had taken place in the village, the one that had earned the colonel his reputation.

It was a big day in the marketplace. The *caïd* and his brother were shot down right there in the *souk*. The country people scattered, racing down the roads, pushing their donkeys and mules in front of them. Many of them left their beasts behind so they could get away even faster. But the *harkis* and French soldiers, who were transported in jeeps and trucks, caught up with everybody. Kicks, rifle blows, abuse and threats as far as the barracks from which some never returned.

Hassan started for home with his friend Tayeb. A *harki* named Jahnout, known for his bad temper, yelled at them, machine gun at the ready:

"Over here, you sons of bitches! You pretend you don't know anything! I'll settle that for you right now!"

He gave them a couple of kicks in the stomach with his combat boots. Both boys fell into a ditch. He took aim at them, stamped his feet, and hollered, "I'm going to sew up your bellies, you future *fellagas*, if you don't tell me where the *fellaga* went."

Hassan was as white as a sheet, and Tayeb was crying hot tears, swearing he didn't know a thing. The two children were delivered from Jahnout's hands thanks to the intervention of a French policeman. Tayeb cried all the way home. When the time came to leave Hassan to go to his parents' house, he said through his sniffles:

"One day I'll be a *harki* too, and I'll have my revenge on Jahnout."

When Tayeb became a *harki*, he was seventeen. He signed up at the same time as about a dozen other youths, most of them orphans who were on their own and had no money. Hassan was astonished to see his comrade, three years older than himself, decked out in a French army uniform that was too long for him and too big for his adolescent body with its awkward gait.

The recruiter for the *harkis*, a civilian, had a glass eye that was blue and a good eye that was black. He went around bare-headed in the French manner, but on the day of the Aïd festival, he elegantly coiled a turban around his head, one of such sparkling white that it gave him a pious and respectable look. When he wasn't in the café hunched over a game of dominoes, he roamed through the streets and paths of the village giving smiles and greetings right and left. In the evening he would secretly return to the police station to give his report. When he spotted a young man he thought was a possible recruit, he would take a walk with him outside the village. "Listen, son, think about what I've just told you. . . .You get a regular salary at the end of each month; you can get married. When your wife gives birth, you will have money and allowances for the children. And let's face facts: it isn't hard work. Now and then a jaunt here and a little trip there. . . . Who can offer you such an opportunity? What people will say? What do you care what they say! Anyway, they won't dare say a word. So what? Here it's France that gives the orders, and when you wear that uniform, you are France."

Tayeb was no longer the same person. He looked straight ahead when he walked by. He spoke to no one. Even when he ran into Hassan, his playmate only yesterday, he acted as though he did not recognize him. And Hassan, for his part—for reasons he could not explain—felt, from then on, incapable of going up to him. He walked right by him pretending not to see him. The other *harkis* wore their uniform with a certain arrogance, spoke in loud tones, laughed noisily, and went openly to the bistro.

The new recruits got their orders from the newly promoted

sergeant Jahnout. Jahnout's superior was a blond legionnaire, smooth-faced and smiling. The *harki's* post was situated at the west entry to the village across from the police station. Kids would go to watch when the *harkis* got into their trucks, disciplined under the gaze of their commanding officer, but shoving and insulting one another as soon as his back was turned.

Jahnout wanted to marry his cousin Malika. When his mother went to the little village, the *douar*, to ask for the girl's hand, her brother said: "I will never marry my sister to a *harki*. Your son has dishonored us enough."

The poor woman did not insist. She left her sister's house with a heavy heart. She did everything she could to persuade her son to choose a wife from another family. Jahnout refused to listen to her. He hurried off to see his cousin and to tell him that he would pay for his contempt.

"I know you're working with the *fellagas*."

The two families stopped seeing each other. Months went by. Malika was asked for in marriage by a farmer from a nearby hamlet.

Since the beginning of the war, marriage, birth, and circumcision were no longer celebrated with a party. No dancing, no singing, no ululating, no noisy doings of any sort. Close relatives were brought together, and the ceremony took place with the greatest discretion. Hassan had come with his mother. He played by the gully all afternoon. In the evening he ate his couscous in a big wooden dish set on a small table in a storeroom where the other boys had gathered. A sour-faced adolescent was supposed to keep an eye on them. He hit them over the head with a long switch if they shoved each other or laughed too loudly. The smaller children were in a room reserved for the women. The men were in a neighboring house. Abdallah, the bride's brother, took them their dinner. He made no noise going from one house to the other. The silence of the night was disturbed only by the croaking of frogs in the gully.

Jahnout and his men had come up the river bed walking in the sand without any light. He had badgered his commanding officer, the legionnaire, to get permission to go do some close monitoring of that *douar* where things were happening every night. He posted men behind the dense hedges of the gardens, in front of the doors of the houses.

The children sent their empty plates back to the kitchen, then stretched out on a mat. The boy watching them threw a heavy woolen blanket over them. Huddled one against the other, they began to tell riddles, being sure not to raise their voices. The adolescent leaned back against a mule's packsaddle and took out a cigarette butt that he lit from the flame of the lamp. After putting the small children to bed, the women made a circle to paint the bride with henna, to look at her trousseau, and to fix her hair and dress her. In the house next door, the men, wrapped in their burnooses, were smoking and drinking coffee as they exchanged terse words.

After coffee, Abdallah took the coffeepot and went to see the women who had done the cooking in the house reserved for the women and children. Outside, a night filled with stars and the croaking of frogs. It was just as Abdallah was returning toward the men's house that the shooting let loose, echoing from one cliff to the other like a noise from hell. Ten automatic rifles spitting death on the facades of the little stone houses. The children clung to each other. The boy with the switch got under the packsaddle. The women called to each other by name. The babies, awakened with a start, were screaming as they fought one another under the covers. The men looked at each other, haggard and livid, stammering some prayers. The bride, shaken with sobs, had taken refuge in a corner, her hands and feet still wrapped with the henna strips. Her mother, standing in the doorway, beat her breast with her hands, gasping, "My son! My son! He just went outside. Oh, my God!"

The shooting stopped. The doors were broken in by kicks and rifle blows. Cries, insults, threats, blasphemy. The *harkis* burst into the houses and shoved all the men outside. They tried to get into the women's house, but two old women angrily barred the way, calling them traitors, unnatural sons, and men without modesty. They brought down such terrible curses on their heads that the *harkis* backed away. The men were gathered together under the trees a few yards from Abdallah's body lying on its side. Jahnout emerged from the shadows and walked over to the dead body.

"Don't you know it is forbidden to go out at night? He got what was coming to him. The curfew is the curfew! He's my cousin, but all he had to do was stay put. Tough luck. . . ."

Abdallah's mother came running and pushed the *harki* who tried to keep her from going by. She threw herself on the inani-

31

mate body, and a long cry of pain pierced the night. The men were authorized to go back into the house. They took the dead body inside while one man carried the mother in his arms. Malika tore the henna strips from her hands and threw herself to the ground, scratching at her face.

"My brother! My brother! My brother, son of my mother!"

Then, as if under the spell of madness, she began to tear off everything she was wearing: scarves, belt, earrings, rings. She ripped her dress and her chemise from top to bottom. The women grabbed hold of her and forcibly took her to the next room where she went on howling, looking insane and drained of tears.

The next morning, the men reassembled under the trees. The police were there for the official report. Jahnout, very pale and uneasy under the silent look of the farmers, furnished explanations and showed the spot where his cousin had fallen and the garden hedges behind which he had posted his men to take the *fellagas* by surprise. The police verified the identity of the men, then had the mother of Abdallah come out so they could question her. Jahnout was to serve as interpreter.

"Traitor!"

She spat in his face. He jumped back, frightened. A policeman gave the woman a shove and ordered her to keep quiet.

"Unbeliever! I could cut you to pieces and my heart wouldn't be satisfied. The uniform you're wearing won't protect you very long. . . ."

The farmers begged her not to say anything more.

Two of Malika's uncles came into the women's house after the police had gone away. The oldest, leaning on a cane, spoke in a quiet voice, and tears rolled gently down his cheeks.

"Our son is dead. God alone is the master of our destinies, and we are his slaves. What could we do, my daughters? Our son is dead, and our affliction is terrible. In spite of everything, let the marriage take place, because it is in the plans of the Lord. Let us not oppose His will. Dress the girl. We will lead her to the dwelling of her spouse."

Malika refused to take off the clothes she had reduced to tatters. They had to use force to dress her and to get her to leave the house. "I don't want to go. Leave me with my brother! May bad fortune rain on your heads!"

On the little square of the *douar*, she fell to the ground at the very spot where her brother had fallen. She clawed at the earth, pulling up clods that she smeared over her mouth. They got her to her feet with difficulty. But she fell down to the earth again, on her knees. Then one of the uncles came up with a stick in his hand, and he began to beat her, his teeth pressed against his lips. The women were crying. The men looked haggard. The children stood staring and dazed. Hassan clenched his fists in his pockets, his nails biting into the flesh. His eyes filled with tears. He ran away, crossing the gully, and threw himself down behind a haystack. He pressed his hands to his eyes, and everything began to turn in his head: Malika, the uncle brandishing the stick, the white veil, the trees, the houses, all deformed, cracked and dismembered by pain. He relaxed his brows, and tears poured down his cheeks, violent and liberating.

The men took turns carrying the bride in their arms. Malika huddled in a corner and remained prostrate all day long. But at twilight, outwitting everybody, she ran off barefoot and got back to the house of her parents by going through the ravines. The next morning the uncles, confused and disoriented, dragged her forcibly back to the house of her husband. But she got away again, and they all finally agreed that this marriage was not to take place. The girl's family returned part of the dowry to the boy's family, then they walked away saying: "God did not wish this marriage. Let us submit to His will. May He be praised for everything!"

Smaïl, the former shepherd, enterprising and a good shot, had been named corporal-in-chief. In the village, rumor had it that he had killed Abdallah. He defended himself. He'd had nothing to do with that murder: Jahnout had given the *harkis* the order to open fire. The partisans got in touch with Smaïl, who made no trouble when they asked him to pay a fine and to hand over some ammunition. Then one night in July—Jahnout was away—he took an axe and decapitated the legionnaire he caught lying in bed, and rejoined the partisans with arms and ammunition at the head of a group of *harkis*.

The next morning, the *harkis* who had not deserted were arrested, interrogated, and given a beating by the French police assisted by Jahnout, who had been urgently called back. Then they were put out in the sun against the walls of the police station, bareheaded, without belts or shoelaces. Tayeb was among them. People looked at them out of the corner of their eyes as they went by on the street. No one took pity on them. That very evening, all of them except Jahnout were discharged.

"What good are those donkeys! They won't make good French soldiers or good *fellagas*!" cried the colonel with the long pipe.

February 1962

The war was possibly going to end. People who knew how to read bought the newspaper and showed it to those who didn't know how to read as they enumerated the names of the Algerian representatives that could be seen in the photos, well dressed, in good health, smiling.

"God be praised!" people said.

The arrest of Ferhat, a young man eighteen years old who was a native of the valley, reminded everyone that the war was not over yet and that the colonel with the long pipe was not a man to let a terrorist attack go unpunished. Ferhat was responsible for guaranteeing communications between the partisans and the militants in the village. Fear and confusion. Those who had had a direct relationship with him quickly disappeared, melting into anonymity in a neighboring village or burying themselves in the house of a relative who would not be suspected of connivance with the rebels. Hassan's brother-in-law entrusted his wife to his in-laws and went to stay with his cousin who was a *harki* in a village of the region.

Thibaud used electrodes. At dawn, the soldiers encircled the farm. When it got lighter, a helicopter landed in the stadium still covered with snow and picked up the colonel and the stool pigeon hidden under his army blanket. Useless precaution: everyone knew who was under the blanket.

"May misfortune fall on his head! He has already sold out his brothers!" said Fatim-Zohra, her eyes glued to the helicopter as it took to the air.

A short time later, two yellow planes appeared over the village. They flew in a circle, then went off toward the valley. The blast of the first bombs resounded. There had never been a bombardment so close to the village before. Usually it was far off in the somber blue mountains. It was so far away that the planes were invisible. But sometimes, when the light was less brilliant, the phosphorescent balls could be counted as they fell to earth.

Everybody looked in the direction of the valley. The French were on their balconies. The captain's wife took aim with her field glasses. Children were ensconced on hilltops. In their ceaseless rounds, the yellow planes made ever larger circles until they were over the village. The children followed their flight in silence. Neither mad cries nor greetings accompanied hand-waves to the pilots as was the custom. Hassan's mother, standing back of the window, was crying.

"They're going to kill them all! After that, it's our turn."

Malek, sitting on the window sill, feverishly watched the appearance of the planes.

They said that the Old Man, as on every other day, had awakened at the first cock's crow. He had gently pushed back his covers. His young wife, face toward the wall and arm around her baby, was still sleeping. He went into the common room. Yemmouna, his first wife, came to meet him. He bowed. She placed a kiss on his head and handed him a pitcher. He went outside and walked softly around the house. He stopped several times, listening to the silence and scrutinizing the neighborhood. He squatted in his habitual place under the fig tree and did his ablutions.

"Master, you look worried," Yemmouna said to him when he came back in.

"Woman, go wake up the sleepers. Tell them to leave immediately, through the ravine of asphodels. The kid has sold us out. They're all around us in the shadows."

The house resounded with noises, questions, and the crying of children. Everyone gathered around the Old Man.

"Go through the ravine of asphodels. Everything else is cut off."

"And you, Master," timidly asked the young wife clasping her baby who was suckling her.

"It's true, Father. We can't leave you here alone," the men said in their turn.

"The ravine of asphodels isn't a path for me."

"Go quickly!" said Yemmouna.

"There are the planes, Mama!" shouted Malek from his observation post.

Hassan, stretched out on his back, was listening.

. . .

One sweltering day in June, Hassan, shirt open to his chest, went to steal some tender ears of corn in a neighboring field. It was Thursday, market day. The crowd of shoppers, peddlers, and idlers was beginning to disperse when two yellow planes approached the village. They began to fly in circles so low that the silhouettes of the pilots could be seen when the planes swerved overhead. They had never before flown over the village at that altitude. Ordinarily, they went over very high—so high, in fact, that they resembled tiny black or shining points trailing a white stream behind them that disappeared as they went off into the distance.

"Jets! Jets!" cried the children who sometimes couldn't see them at all, but only heard the muffled rumbling in the sky.

Hassan had started to run like an idiot. They're going to drop bombs on the village. Nothing will be left but ruins. Cabrane had described to him the missions of planes during the war. That was what they did to release their cargo of bombs. Cabrane still had shrapnel in his flesh. His blood was slowly carrying them toward his heart. Hassan went into the wheat field and crossed it, panting. On the other side there was an enormous rock that stuck out like a platform under which he used to play. Hassan coiled up in a craggy corner of the rock, took a deep breath, spat in front of himself, and then straightened up in fright: a black rat, eyes afire, was looking at him. Hassan jumped up and began to run again in the direction of his parents' house. His mother was praying, her hands open on her stomach as if to protect the child she was carrying.

Lahcen, the older brother, was laughing and turning in pirouettes, arms apart, as though he were a plane, going as far as the door to look up at the sky, and laughing still.

"That scares you! Look what I'm going to do to them, just like in the movies!"

Then, arms outstretched, fists closed, he unleashed an imaginary machine gun in the direction of the planes.

"Stop acting like a fool. They might see you."

"There they are! There they are, Mama! Come on, you planes! Come on down on our house!" cried Malek from the top of his perch.

"Be quiet, son! All they need is to hear you yelling."

They said that the Old Man and Yemmouna were sitting on either side of the fireplace. A coffeepot with a long spout was boiling over the fire. The Old Man was drinking his third cup of coffee when the colonel, Ferhat, without his blanket on, and a dozen French soldiers and *harkis* burst into the room. The Old Man looked up. Ferhat looked away.

"On your feet! Come here!"

The Old Man was wearing all of his military decorations, and Yemmouna was clasping a red scarf tied by the four corners. The colonel took it from her.

"That belongs to my daughters and my daughters-in-law."

He unfolded the scarf and examined the contents with

curiosity: some silver jewelry, a scented soap, and two or three flasks of perfume.

Ferhat led the colonel to the room where the grain was stored. It was separated from the living quarters and had a second door that opened out onto the orchard. One of the soldiers took out his dagger and cut open the sacks of grain lined up against the wall one after the other. The sound of the grain that spread out at his feet filled the soldier with childish jubilation. The colonel had a serious look. As soon as they approached the farm, he had had a premonition that the foxes were no longer in the burrow. Ferhat went toward the corner where the saddlebags were stacked. He pushed them aside.

"It's there."

Then, stooping down, he lifted up a wood panel covered with a layer of earth that was the same color as the floor of the room. The soldiers stepped back. Nothing moved in the hidding place. Thibaud handed a flashlight to a *harki*. The man stretched out flat on his stomach at the edge of the black hole and swept the interior of the hiding place with a stream of light. He shook no with his head and stood up. The colonel ordered Ferhat and the Old Man to climb down into the refuge and to hand up everything they found down there. Ferhat went first, an electric lamp in his hand. The Old Man followed with difficulty. Yemmouna was crying as she watched them slowly go down into the earth. Ferhat handed up some blankets, some canned goods, two hunting rifles with the barrels rusted, an alarm clock, several pairs of clogs, a transistor, some cigarette cartons, a few toilet articles, and some old newspapers. Two *harkis* went down into the hiding place in their turn, followed by Thibaud and the colonel. The colonel rapidly inspected the place and came back up with his jaws clenched. He was holding the Old Man's military decorations in his hand.

They said that at the very moment the young man put his lips to the Old Man's right shoulder to ask his pardon, Thibaud had fired a burst with his machine gun. The two fell side by side without a cry or a jerk. Thibaud was the last to climb out; he turned around and threw in a grenade. The soldiers left the farm. The yellow planes nose-dived. Yemmouna left along the gully, her red scarf tied by the four corners over her arm. The earth was trembling beneath her feet.

It was during those days of snow, cold, and anguish that Youssef, Hassan's father, giving in to panic, strangled Ouarda. She was reddish colored and affectionate. She resembled their first dog.

One summer morning a rumor somehow got started that French soldiers were going to go into every house to kill the dogs whose untimely nocturnal barking kept them from passing unnoticed and surprising the partisans stopping in the village. Ouarda had just had a litter. She was left one puppy that had been destined for some neighbors. That particular morning, Hassan was learning the Koran at the mosque when his younger brother, his face flushed from running, found the teacher and begged him, in the name of his mother, to excuse his brother for an urgent matter.

Hassan found his mother very upset, standing in the middle of the courtyard with the dog on a leash and the puppy in a basket at her feet.

"God bless and keep you, my son! Quick, take the dog to your uncle's house. They say French soldiers are going to every house to kill the dogs."

Hassan, who loved Ouarda and his uncle's house, took hold of the leash. Fatiha took the basket with the puppy that, separated from its mother, began to whine. The path descended abruptly into the fields. Ouarda strained against the leash, constantly turning to see if her little one was following her. Fatiha trotted along at a distance in back of them. Hassan, forehead all sweaty, did not stop swearing at her and the dog. He wanted to run still faster. It was as though the soldiers were on his heels and could catch up with him from one minute to the next.

The two children got to the uncle's house tired and covered with dust. They drank some buttermilk, ate some hard-boiled eggs with salted butter, then went back to their mother feeling proud of their adventure. But the next day Ouarda, radiantly happy, reappeared, held on the leash by the elder cousin. The younger one held the puppy in his arms. The uncle had refused to keep the dog; he wanted no trouble with the partisans, who also were concerned with going about at night unnoticed.

Ouarda filled the night with her barking, bothering a lot of neighbors. Youssef got a lot of complaints.

"Dogs are made for barking," commented Fatim-Zohra.

One day, a woman neighbor with little affection for Fatim-Zohra told Youssef that the partisans insisted on the death of the dog. Youssef said nothing to his wife, because he knew what her response would be: "Why is it only our dog that bothers the partisans? There are dozens of dogs in the village, and they all bark at night!" Shortly after that, Fatim-Zohra went to take care of a daughter who had just had a baby. Taking advantage of her absence, the woman neighbor took up the cudgel again.

"It seems the brothers have talked more about you. They told me: 'If he refuses to kill the dog, we'll take care of it.' Me, I'm just telling you what I was told, and you, do what you please. If you're looking for complications, that's your business."

That evening when he got home, Youssef looked very serious. He mechanically distributed oranges to the children seated around the fire, then went out to the shed where the dog was tied up. Contrary to his usual practice, he carried no bone that night. After a few minutes he came back in. His eyes were wet, and his hands were trembling. He did his ablutions, slipped on his burnoose and sat on his prayer rug. For a long while he invoked God's mercy. He went to bed without supper, and that night Ouarda troubled no one's sleep.

Hassan takes Ouarda in his arms. He runs through the night, snapped at by a pack of wolfhounds sent by the soldiers. He goes as fast as the wind, but the watchdogs are as fast as he. They are just about to catch him. Ouarda is changed into a winged dog, and Hassan finds himself on her back. The wolfhounds are transformed into soldiers pointing their long rifles at the sky. They open fire, but Hassan and Ouarda are very high in the night, up near the stars. Then Ouarda separates herself from Hassan and becomes a star that disappears in the multitude of constellations. Hassan struggles as if he were drowning. He falls into the void, and for the moment, nothing can hold him back or save him. The anguish of dislocation. He plunges into a liquid mass: a pool, a river, a sea. He continues to descend, the prisoner of an irrepressible turmoil. The anguish became unbearable. Hassan groaned and awakened. But his fear, almost palpable, was still at his side, filling the entire silent house. Hassan suddenly pulled up the covers and curled up, his heart beating wildly.

Hassan calmed down. He was still thinking about Ouarda. At dawn, on his way to work, his father would drag her to the edge of the road. A bit later on, the garbage collectors would throw her on their truck, without a word of pity, no doubt even grumbling unhappily. It's easier to lift up a garbage pail than the body of a dog that evidently was well fed by its masters. Ouarda was going off to join Ouarda the First, the one that was killed by soldiers during the great raid.

The dog barked furiously at the three soldiers who had just jumped into the courtyard after walking across the roof of the house. She was lunging on her chain at the door of the shed. One of the soldiers went up to her, machine gun at the ready. The father took Malek in his arms and went over to the soldier whose intentions he could guess. Perhaps the sight of the baby would evoke some humanity in the soldier's heart. The soldier tried to fire; the weapon seemed to resist him. Youssef bent down to the dog to quiet it, but nothing would do: she continued her racket against the intruders.

"Let go of her!"

One of the soldiers, conciliatory, tapped his comrade's shoulder. The shot rang out. The bullet went through the dog's neck. The baby clung to his father. Then the whole family was shoved outside by the soldiers. The mother had just enough time to hold a burnoose out to her husband, another to her son, and to cover her shoulders with a veil.

On the road under the guard of a horde of soldiers that had come to the village during the night, a dense crowd of men, women, and children walked along in silence. The men and adolescent boys were directed toward the stadium; the women and children, toward the nearby slaughterhouses.

The village was totally emptied of its inhabitants. The slaughterhouses were soon filled up. Nevertheless, the soldiers continued to force in more women and children. The boys, delighted at finding themselves all together in such a strange place, forgot the gravity of the moment. They hung from the bars and hooks, turned on the water spigots, and exchanged blows and invectives as they climbed onto the roof of the red wagon that served as transportation for the meat. The women with their babies and daughters looked pale and defeated. Some of them were crying—those who were afraid they would never again see their son, husband, brother, or father. Others were talking, asking questions, saying prayers. Hassan, leaning against a door the color of blood, was thinking about Ouarda lying in her shed with her mouth wide open. The small children were hungry. They began to cry and to ask for any kind of food. Some of the women were generous dividing the little they had with their neighbors' children as well as their own, while others, hardened by their selfishness and greed, turned a deaf ear.

That afternoon the women and children were authorized to return to their homes. Nevertheless, before they were allowed to leave, their genitals had to be checked: God only knows what could be hidden under that heap of rags and veils. Two Frenchwomen, strangers to the village, felt between their legs.

The villagers found their houses turned completely inside out: bedding overthrown, coffers and wardrobes wide open, dishware and legal papers thrown on the floor. Fatim-Zohra could not find her silver jewelry in the yellow-striped lacquered box. Hassan went to look for the wheelbarrow where, with his mother's help, he had placed the dog. He pushed the wheelbarrow to the edge of a wheat field. Jeha, the son of neighbors, pickax over his shoulder like a workman on his way to a construction site, followed him. Once Ouarda was covered with earth, snout pointing toward Mecca, the two boys planted an oblong stone at each end of the tomb.

Jeha stretched out in the wheelbarrow, looked up at the sky, and said, "Dogs and cats have seven souls. The soldier who killed Ouarda will be tortured by Azrael as though he killed seven men. Azrael's cudgel will break his bones."

Jeha began to laugh. Hassan, seated on the embankment, said nothing. He was looking into the distance toward the side of the mountain at the little cemetery among the nettles where his grandmother lay. "Ouarda may meet my grandmother in paradise."

Hassan was convinced that his grandmother was settled in paradise among the blessed. She left behind only sincere grief. People said she was a woman of good, with a compassionate heart and a helping hand. Her snowy shroud was one she prepared herself while she was alive, one brought back from Mecca, the blessed land, by a pilgrim. They said that a week before her death, she had had a vision foretelling her destiny and that of the country.

"I'm going to be leaving soon," she said one morning to her daughter-in-law. "They came to look for me during the night, all of the dead whose names and faces I know: my mother, my father, my children, my brothers, my sisters, my cousins, my uncles, my aunts, my grandparents. . . . They came out of their tombs all dressed in white. 'What are you doing here?' I asked them. 'This land will know seven good harvests. There will be so much wheat and barley that the silos will be overflowing! So much wheat and barley! We will leave our tombs; they will serve to store the surplus. Come with us. Put on this white robe.' And since I refused, my mother stepped forward. She tore the dress I was wearing. Then, taking a flask of musk out of her breast, she poured it on my head. 'Where are you going?' I said to them as I stood there in my new robe. 'Up to the mountain to prepare your wedding.' And God opened my eyes. I am going to leave, my daughter. God keep you! The hard times are not far off. I am going to leave soon."

Hassan must have been six. She died suddenly in the night. He slept by her side so he could listen to her stories. In the morning, she was washed by two elderly village women at one end of the courtyard in back of two zinc plaques set at an angle. The water from the ablutions ran under the front door. The children stepped over the little stream, being careful not to wet their feet: water from the dead causes sores that never can be cured! Under the frightened look of his comrades, Hassan plunged his feet several times into the little stream.

The grandmother was laid out on a green stretcher lent by the mosque. A red wool blanket was laid over the body wrapped in white. Four men placed the stretcher on their shoulders, and the cortege took the path toward the mountain. Everyone invoked God's mercy with a great droning noise that gave Hassan cold chills. They disappeared high up behind the almond trees. Hassan sat down on a rock at the foot of a wall. He didn't have to wait long. Soon they reappeared. They were no longer singing, and they were all running as if from sudden panic, while the stretcher bounced on the backs of two of the porters.

That was the way things always were after a burial. Hassan knew that. As soon as the dead person is under the ground, the living take off and hurry to return to their own kind. Because as soon as the dead body is buried, it returns to life, and then comes out of the tomb in the hope of capturing a living person to take with it to the other world.

"Jeha, why do the men run away after they've buried the dead?" Hassan asked his comrade still lying in the wheelbarrow.

"Because they're afraid. Me, I'm not afraid of the dead. When my cows go into the cemetery, I let them go. One time, I even found a bone, like that, when I was walking among the tombs."

The men were not set free. They stayed in the stadium, which had been encircled with a high barbed wire enclosure put up by the prisoners. March nights are cold. The women and children huddled under their blankets. They kept an ear cocked for noises outside, and whispered words permeated with fear.

The families were given permission to send blankets and food to the prisoners. But if the blankets and the burnooses, thrown in a ball over the barbed wire, did get to the prisoners— and rarely to the ones they were destined for—coffee, little cakes, fruit, and tobacco went directly into the tents of the soldiers. The children quickly got to know the *harkis*. They made a circle around them and asked them what was going to happen to the men.

"Don't be afraid, children. Tomorrow morning you'll get your parents back. And now, go tell your mothers to prepare a bit of cake and coffee for us. We're your brothers, Arabs like you."

"Let them drink poison!" answered the women.

To tell the truth, the boys were happy to find themselves alone with the women, rid of their fathers. Hassan acted as head of the family. He was the man his mother could count on. He gave orders to his sisters and kept watch over the garden, and in the evening, once he had closed all the doors to the house, he stretched out in his father's place, with the lamp and matches beside him.

Every day, the eyes of the women and children turned toward the stadium. The men were still behind barbed wire. Sad and silent, the village seemed devoid of all life. The children no longer played, and Mohand Akli, left at liberty because he was crazy, sang no more. In the houses, provisions began to run out. Accompanied by Abla, the daughter of neighbors, Hassan went to his father's grocery to look for a bit of food. They were very much afraid as they went down the village's main street with all the shop doors shut, all rooms in the cafés transformed into military encampments. But as soon as they were alone in the store, behind a locked door, they talked about marriage.

"I will buy you a ring."

"Only a ring!"

"Two, if you wish."

"I want earrings, all in gold."

She took him by the neck, and he pushed her back on the bench. She neither struggled nor protested. Her black eyelashes were blinking rapidly. He stretched out on top of her, and pressed the lower part of his body against hers, his face crimson.

"How much will you give me the first night? You won't hurt me. . . . Let me see."

He complied. She began to laugh.

"About like a sausage!"

"And you?"

"If you look, you'll lose your sight."

"I've already seen my sister's."

"You should be ashamed!"

. . .

It was only on the seventh day that the men were set free. They went slowly home, their clothes splotched with mud, their faces swollen, their eyes dull. The children went ahead to meet them, kiss them and relieve them of the burnooses and blankets they were carrying. The old women came out to meet them as well. They kissed them and, their voices choked with emotion, praised God for having returned them alive to their families. But not all of the men came home, and those who did not return that day never did come back.

The spring of the following year, Abla was taken to the cemetery on the mosque's green wheelbarrow, Abla poisoned by her brother, people said in a low voice. Hassan was left dumbfounded by the news of the death. Just the night before, he had seen her in her red dress, a wicker basket in her hand. She was going toward the fields, probably to get some seasonal herbs that her sister-in-law doted on.

"What happened?"

"God preserve us! We're not busybodies, but they say her brother killed her with rat poison."

"God preserve us!"

"He diluted it with milk. He told her, 'Drink it or I'll cut your throat with this knife.' "

"God preserve us from evil!"

Hassan pretended to be absorbed by his work. In reality, nothing said by the two women escaped him. His mother watched him momentarily out of the corner of her eye. No, he wasn't listening. He was concentrating on finishing up his bow.

"God protect us! You know the girl never stopped wandering around the fields. A roving foot never comes home clean. The *harki* was in the ravine. People say it was a *harki*. Who knows what he was doing there. There was a she-mule in the ravine as well. I think he was riding it, the repulsive brute. God curse him! He grabbed her. He said, 'If you cry, I'll cut your throat!' That's how misfortune comes."

"God protect us!"

"When she got back to the house, her legs were covered with blood, and her brother's wife began to claw at her own face. God preserve us! We aren't gossipers, but they say she put her fingers in to see for herself. 'You have dishonored us, you devil's spawn! May death take you!' The girl was crying. Then the brother arrived."

"And the mother?"

"The poor thing was in her corner. She was crying in silence. She has enough with her illness. She's at death's door."

"He shut her up in a room. He took off his belt and began to beat her. He was like a crazy man. There was blood all over. She was on her knees. She begged him. He went to get a knife, and he said, 'I am going to cut her throat. I'm going to cut her throat right now!' And his wife said to him, "No, stop! You'll end up in prison.' Then he went to look for the rat poison. He poured it into a bowl of milk. He said, 'Drink or I'll cut your throat.' She said, 'Yes, yes, I'll drink, my brother, I'll drink. I'll do whatever you want, my brother.' And she drank, she drank."

"Oh my God! My God!"

"They say her whole body turned violet. And you know, they

didn't even wash her! They put her that way in the shroud, like that. It's a sin! And then they told people, 'Abla died during the night. She had terrible stomach convulsions. She must have eaten some kind of poisonous herbs.' "

"God take her soul!"

Fatim-Zohra turned her head toward her son; he was crying, his broken bow lying in front of him.

Hassan hid his briefcase behind a bush and returned to the pathway. He wasn't going to school that afternoon. The sun beat straight straight down on his head. He wasn't thinking about anything. He was satisfied just to follow the thread of the path, invisible in places under the thick grass. He stopped at a fountain where a woman, breathless, her forehead covered with perspiration, was kneading a pile of wool. He had a drink, threw some water on his face, and inquired, "Does this path go to the cemetery?"

"Which cemetery?"

"The Nobles' resting place."

"But why do you want to go to the Nobles' resting place, my child? Whose son are you?"

"I have no parents," said Hassan without knowing why he was lying.

And he went on his way. The woman turned her head and went on with her work. The pathway went higher and higher. There were no houses—only stones, grass, prickly shrubs, a few scrawny almond trees, some junipers and, on the foothills of the mountain, a herd of sheep.

The path disappeared into a vast sloping terrain, also full of rocks and shrubs. Was that the cemetery where Abla had been buried? Hassan had trouble making out the tombs. He had never seen a cemetery up close before. He went forward slowly, almost staggering. The alignment of certain stones struck him: probably the most recent graves. And Abla's grave? He continued to advance, as though he could do nothing else. And the cemetery spread out before him until it was measureless. Where are its limits? Perhaps it has none.

The notes of a flute suddenly filled the air. Hassan stopped and looked around him: there was nothing but the stones and shrubs baking in the sun. And Abla's grave? The sun dazzled him. He blinked his eyes. A red figure came toward him out of the sunlight. It was Abla, draped in a red robe, a wicker basket in her hand, her eyes blindfolded with a blue scarf like the one she wore when they played blindman's buff on the road. The modulations of the flute seemed to well up from inside himself. Her lips moved: "Come, Hassan." Hassan made a half-turn and left. Someone came running after him, someone whose breathing he could hear. He ran through the rocks and shrubbery as he had never run before. He wanted to cry out, but he couldn't. "Stop, stop, you bastard! Son of a bitch!" and stones began to rain all around him. Hassan looked in the direction of the cries. Up on a bluff, two shepherds, armed with slingshots, were making him their target. Hassan ran on down the path like a madman. A stone hit him on the heel. He didn't stop till he reached the fountain. The woman was no longer there, but many pieces of wool were floating in the basin. He drank greedily, then sat down on the edge of the basin to wash his bloodstained foot and shoe. He put his head under the running water, drank again and, calmed down, went on his way, one foot shod, the other bare.

March 1962

Hassan's brother, a black suitcase in hand and dressed in uniform, came home one night. Picked up in a police roundup in Paris, Lahcen had first been sent to prison for insubordination.

The French authorities had been looking for him for some time. To the French police who interrogated him regularly about his son's workplace, Youssef would reply, "Look, Chief, how can I give you my son's address? I don't know where he is. My son's a good-for-nothing, I tell you. I sent him to France to find work to help me bring up my children. Just see the results: not even a letter to tell me how things are going."

After time in prison, Lahcen had been sent to a barracks in Algiers to shape him up.

"A driver's license is a good thing, my son," said the father as he brushed away the grains of couscous stuck to his mustache. "That way, the day you get out of the army, you'll easily find work. A person with a trade never dies of hunger. I'm telling you."

Silence. The father watched his children getting warm at the fire. They were talking among themselves and laughing. In a confidential tone, he added, "And the others, my son? I hope you think about that too."

"I do what I can," murmured Lahcen.

Hassan, who heard every bit of the quiet exchange of words, admired his brother even more. "I know secrets too, secrets I keep to myself. I saw the letters of the FLN, and I saw the seal they use, a red rectangle with the words: 'Political Commissioner.'"

One evening Hassan got an urgent call from his brother-in-law who handed him three open envelopes.

"Read these letters and tell me who they're addressed to. Also tell me the total amount that's marked on it."

Hassan had done the reading, feeling full of gratitude to his brother-in-law for the confidence he had shown in him. The first letter was addressed to the colonial administrator of the village, and the other two to *harkis*. The brother-in-law, a secret Resistance fighter, was supposed to take these letters to their destinations. But as he had inadvertently mixed them up, and did not know how to read, he had called in Hassan so he would not commit a blunder.

Another day, Hassan had been taken aside by one of his father's cousins, a *bon vivant* who secretly went to the French bistro.

"Here, little cousin, read this letter for me. I trust you."

The paper was marked with a red rectangular seal with the

following words: "Political Commissioner," which Hassan did not understand. The text, however, was quite clear: the addressee was asked to pay a fine of ten thousand francs, and was ordered to stop drinking. A recurrence would exact a more serious punishment.

"Do you know how much I earn, little cousin? Twenty thousand francs a month. . . . So, let's order two lemonades to forget life's miseries."

The two brothers put on their burnooses and slipped side by side under the heavy woolen blankets. The rest of the family slept in the next room.

"My barrack is just across from the hospital, the big hospital. You've already heard of Mustafa Hospital. I'll come to see you often."

"You didn't bring a revolver back with you?"

"A revolver!"

"Well, yes. Some kind of weapon! All soldiers are armed."

"I have a knife."

"Switchblade or a dagger?"

"Switchblade."

"Let's see."

"I'll show you tomorrow."

Lahcen, tired from his journey, fell asleep right away. Hassan was thinking about the knife. He liked knives. He always had a knife on him. It gave him a feeling of strength. Once when a strong boy had wanted to beat him up, Hassan took a knife with a wooden handle out of his pocket. He clutched it in his hand, jaws clenched. His attacker backed up against a wall. Hassan held the point of the blade against the boy's navel.

"Take your knife away. I just wanted to kid you."

"Swear you won't bother me any more."

"I swear by God."

Hassan let him go. The boy went some twenty yards, then turned around and shouted:

"If you're a man, come fight with your fists, but don't worry. I'll catch you one day without your knife."

His brother encouraged him to fight with boys of his own age. He did not intervene, but encouraged him with his shouting and his advice: "Butt him, punch him, right fist, now the left, knee to the groin, now trip him, that's it, bravo!" Hassan fought with spirit and won. His brother carried him on his shoulders and ran. But then one day Lahcen went off to France. By himself, however, Hassan lost his confidence and didn't know how to fight any more.

When Lahcen returned from France four years later, Hassan was so happy to see him that he began to cry, puzzling those around him by that sign of weakness associated with women.

Lahcen's return had not pleased their father. Not only had the son not mailed back any money, he had come home with nothing but a small valise. Youssef was embarrassed. He was ashamed of his son. Everybody coming home from France comes back with suitcases full of clothes for the family, and money in their pockets; why else go to France? He couldn't understand why his son had not acted like everybody else. He racked his brains and finally concluded, "My son is young and handsome, but he's an imbecile. He must have got himself robbed on the boat or getting off the boat. That's why he returned empty-handed."

Once the joys of homecoming were over, Lahcen began to yawn with boredom. One afternoon after trying in vain to take a nap, he got up with a sigh, stood back against the wall, wiped his clammy forehead, took a deep breath, and spoke to Fatim-Zohra, who was sewing on the threshold across from him.

"Mama, if you don't get me married right away, I'll go back to France next week, and for a long while this time."

That very evening, Fatim-Zohra got permission from her husband to look for a wife for her son. It wasn't difficult. She happened to know all the marriageable girls in the village and in the vicinity. She particularly liked Zahia, an eighteen-year-old country girl, thin and lively. The two fathers met in the café, and the marriage was decided. The merchant who was supplying the bride's trousseau quickly consented to credit. Lahcen would send the money from France a little later on.

The bride, hidden behind a veil and accompanied by two women and a young girl, arrived in a taxi. A neighbor took her in his arms and carried her to the door of the house. Fatim-Zohra greeted her with a discreet ululation, just one, because it was improper to express joy in such painful times. The following day at dawn, Lahcen sent a friend to Hassan to find out in which room he would join his wife. Between brothers, one could not talk directly about things concerning sex.

"I think she'll be in the room to the left."

The messenger duly communicated the information, but Lahcen sent him back to his brother for more precise details.

"When you say to the left, what does that mean? Is it on the left when you come into the house or when you leave? There's left on the one side, and a left on the other side. Everything depends on the direction you're looking. You understand what I mean? Right now, you and I are looking at each other. So, your left is my right! And my left is your right!"

"It's the room without a window."

Hassan was mistaken, because at the very last minute, the women decided that the nuptial night would take place in the other room, one that was bigger, more comfortable and with a window. There was, nevertheless, neither confusion nor hesitation: when the groom, his package of peanuts under his arm, pushed open the front door, an old aunt went up to him and perfunctorily pointed out to him the room where his wife was waiting. Hassan and his father spent the night at a neighbor's house.

The next morning, Hassan, feeling rather embarrassed and not knowing where to look, ventured into the house. The women surrounded the bride, looking very pale, who was vomiting into a basin.

Ten days later on, Lahcen left for France again. Zahia, looking paler than ever, fell sick. Her parents came to get her. Her mother took care of her. She did get well but did not go back to her in-laws' house.

"I don't want my daughter to be those people's servant. She

can go back when her husband returns from France."

Informed of the situation by letter, Lahcen answered his father to say that his wife could stay with her parents as long as she wished. He sent money orders to pay for the trousseau, and then, one day, papers to annul the marriage.

The father said, "My son, before leaving for Algiers, why don't you take your brother to the army doctor in the village? People say good things about him. After all, you're a French soldier; you speak French very well. Ask him to write a letter to the doctors in Algiers so they'll take care of your brother."

Hassan hadn't gone out of the house for several weeks. He was pale and thin. As it was cold, his mother covered his shoulders with a white burnoose. As soon as he was outside in the street, he took it off and rolled it up to carry under his arm. The brothers waited in the corridor of the infirmary where soldiers wearing bandages walked by without looking at them. The doctor was tall and had an authoritative voice. He opened Hassan's eyelids. He asked questions in French. The brother translated into Arabic. Hassan answered in Arabic. The brother translated into French.

"Hasn't your brother ever gone to school?"

"Yes, Captain. He has a certificate and is continuing his studies at the *lycée* in Sétif."

"Well then, why doesn't he want to answer my questions in French?"

His voice was metallic, accusatory.

Hassan is seated on his little metal valise at the end of the corridor. He has never been on a train before. But many a Saturday or Sunday leaving school, he has gone near the tracks to wait for the train and to exchange signs of friendship with the travelers whose luck he so envied. At the end of half an hour, his brother comes to fetch him. There is a seat empty in the last car. The car is full. The travelers are talking quietly in French. Lahcen, who has no seat, stays in the corridor. Hassan curls up on his seat and, as the train moves away from Sétif, his thoughts go back to the city he loves, to the school where he seems to have left a part of his being.

The public gardens, almost empty, were plunged into an evening silence. Hassan and his friends from school, hands shoved into their pockets, strolled along paths between the trees while awaiting the time to go back to school. Imitating attractive postures learned in the movies, Ben and his acolytes, cigarettes between their lips, were seated on a wooden bench. The two groups pretended not to see each other. All of a sudden, at the end of a pathway appeared a girl in red on skates, cheeks rosy from the cold and arms open. She could have been a mythical bird fallen from the trees. Ben put his cigarette on the bench, stood up, looked all around him, and then darted off toward the girl. He grasped her in his arms, pressed her to him, and violently planted his mouth on hers. The girl struggled, fell to the ground, and began to howl. Ben ran off guffawing, followed by his two companions.

"Don't forget my cigarette!"

Hassan and his friends were able to watch the whole affair from where they were sitting. Pale and stammering with emotion, the parents of the girl pounced on them. Behind them, the girl was crying and wiping her eyes.

"We're not the ones! The ones who did it ran away. But we don't know their names. They're boarders like us at the *lycée*."

"Where is the *lycée*?"

"Over there, beyond the garden."

"Oh you children! We aren't from around here. We just came from France a week ago."

The woman's sobs welled up in her throat as she spoke.

Hassan and his friends looked very upset as they found their way back to school.

"After all, they're nothing but Frenchmen! We shouldn't have squealed on our friends."

"What did Ben do, after all? He just kissed her! He didn't kill her!"

"He'll certainly be kicked out of school."

"So shit on Ben! He's got it coming."

"That'll teach him to turn us in to the supervisor."

During breakfast, two students from the second class came into the younger students' cafeteria. The supervisor, a strongly athletic Algerian who always wore tight-fitting clothes to show off his massive muscles, acted as though he'd seen nothing. With an impenetrable air about them, they stopped at several tables and whispered some secretive words. And there it was, the magical word that made the rounds of the cafeteria, skirting the tables occupied by the French students: "The strike. The hunger strike! Not a touch of bread or milk or jam." Most of the students were hearing the word for the first time. The strike. There was something festive about that word—a break with the normal order of things. They would stop eating, not as privation imposed from without, but as determination to upset the established order.

A shower of thick gluey slices of bread quickly began to hit the heads of the few who had dared touch the food, either refusing to obey this strangely worded order or simply because they were hungry, as they were every morning. Knives and spoons began to turn in empty bowls. The uproar grew louder and took on the spirit of a joyous revolt. The French, bread in hand, looked around, puzzled and worried.

The boycotting of classes had also been decided. Only the French and a few Algerians, whom their fellow Muslims pierced with hostile looks, lined up before the classrooms. Suddenly an immense clamor arose from the courtyard of the older boys, now thick with people. "With us! Amran! With us! Amran!" The younger boys, who did not know who Amran was nor why these words were being repeated, followed in the older boys' footsteps, delighted at the chance for some horseplay under the very eyes of the proctor standing on his balcony, his indelible red spot on his right temple, the memento of a grenade that had exploded in a movie theater. They said he was sympathetic to the OSA for the good reason that one of his son's favorite games was to run surreptitiously around the corridors of the establishment, at night or early in the morning, inscribing on the walls in red chalk the three letters of fear—letters which, as soon as they were spotted by the Algerians, were the object of ridicule: the Organization of the Secret Army was transformed into the "Organization of Savage Animals."

Hassan finally succeeded in seeing Amran in front of the desk of the general supervisor, between two suitcases and a big bag. He was a high school junior with a very black mustache, a student Hassan knew by sight. He was pale and seemed apart from all the surrounding agitation.

The movement of support for the schoolmate kicked out of the *lycée* increasingly took on the aspect of a sweeping political demonstration. Students cried: "Long live Algeria for Algerians! Long live Ferhat Abbas!" and, on office doors and the walls, between gross phalluses adorned like rockets in flight, flags appeared bearing the star and crescent. At noon the cafeteria was empty. The protesting students sat on the steps in the sun and cheated their hunger with words, magazines, and games. The day students came from home with bread and cakes in their briefcases. They ate happily, and never had food tasted so delicious in Hassan's mouth.

Having no further directives, most students went back to class that afternoon. Others, profiting from the general confusion, went on playing hooky, hiding at the end of corridors, in out-of-the-way stairwells, and in dark corners.

As he went into class, Hassan had the impression of returning from a lofty feat of arms. He was full of assurance, and went straight forward, head high. From above, he sized up those who had shirked the movement, and during class, wholly taken over by the external excitement, he paid no attention to the professor's explanations. Consequently, when the latter surprised him with a question, he was openmouthed. He scratched his head, perplexed, and then, pressed to give an answer, blurted out an inane remark which, in addition to the zero assuring his loss of any outings, earned him the scornful laughter of the traitors.

That night in the dining hall there was a wave of compulsive eating. Everybody—those who had gone on strike and the others as well, probably by emulation—threw themselves on their food with the energy of despair. They scraped their plates, wiped their dishes with bread, and even promptly ate the meatballs, previously so often avoided because of the rumors concerning what went into them. Around the lovely blood-red sauce in which the meatballs were swimming an argument broke out between two former strikers at the table right next to Hassan's. Idel, feeling cheated in his share, brandished his fork at Saci, the head of the table.

"Pass me another spoonful or I'll fix you for good!"

And as Saci did not want to be bothered, his schoolmate ran a tine of his fork into his right nostril. Everyone laughed till they cried, and in the infirmary, where Saci, accompanied by a proctor, appeared with the fork stuck in his nose, the heavy-jowled nurse, a partisan of French Algeria, greeted him with sarcasm.

"Why don't you go to Ferhat Abbas for help," she said with a voice that was hardly charitable, before she stuck a needle into him herself.

In the ranks, as they were getting back to the dormitories, Hassan and his companions stood close behind the French boys whom they had secretly chosen for their sex partners at the beginning of the year. That night their libidos, increased tenfold by their revolutionary passion, were devastating. Messoud, an unbridled little shrimp, got a powerful knee in the spot where he had sinned by going too far too openly.

To most of the students in the dormitories, nights seemed full of danger. There were sexual aggressions perpetrated by discreet, united commandos against deep sleepers or otherwise defenseless students. There were phantoms lurking in the sinks, toilets, and locker rooms.

To have more protection, Hassan carefully tucked in his covers before sliding between the sheets. To avoid going through the dormitory in the dark, he held back his need to urinate, ready to suffer a thousand pains. One night, the need was so great that he had to relieve himself on the tile floor under his bed, lying on his side and letting the urine out in intermittent spurts. The bedside rug, which was quite thick, served as a floorcloth for him and saved him from embarrassment.

. . .

In the dormitory of the sixth grade, nobody liked Lafari. Lafari was at least a head taller than his classmates, and his abdomen—verified the day of the medical appointment—was black with curly hairs. After feeling his testicles with her full hands, the doctor, a woman wearing glasses, said to him with a smile, "I'll make you a bet, my child, that Papa forgot to tell you what year you were born."

If someone made fun of him by alluding to his height, he turned crimson and hit hard. He used his thighs like a vise to imprison the offender.

The matter had begun with a complaint from Lafari's nearest neighbor.

"Monsieur, he stole my pen."

Then, without any previous discussion, a frenzy of accusations gripped the whole school. Poor Lafari was accused of stealing every kind of object, real or imaginary. With all the shoe brushes, tins of shoe wax, towels, belts, bathrobes, shorts, and "baskets" that he supposedly had filched from his poor comrades, there was surely enough to fill a couple of suitcases. As a matter of fact, only the French students had no reproaches for the great thief of the sixth-grade dormitory. To punish the guilty party and cure him forever of his kleptomania, the supervisor, pitiless, decided to inflict on him the supreme insult. Every student, including even those who had made no complaint, stood at the end of their bed in his pajamas, and Lafari, in tears, knelt down before each one of them, imploring their pardon as he called them Monsieur, and made them a pledge that he would steal no more.

II

Algiers. The city was totally dark. It looked deserted to Hassan, clinging to his brother's arm. Each time the glare of a lighthouse pierced the opacity of the shadows, he had the impression that the city was capsizing around him, like a ship whose contours he could not make out.

The Turkish bath gave out an odor of mold coupled with a rancid smell from cooking. The room was bare, the mattress placed right on the cement. The soup was lukewarm; its appearance and its lack of flavor ruined the two brothers' appetite.

"Tomorrow we'll have a good breakfast with croissants," said Lahcen as he lit a cigarette.

Hassan crumpled into a heap, insensitive to the bedbug bites. But he was awakened with a start several times by the noise of explosions. His brother still wasn't asleep. The unknown man on the second floor was still snoring as loudly as ever. Hassan was afraid of the Algiers night.

. . .

Mustafa Hospital, Panasse Pavilion. The orderly spoke with the singsong accent of the South. Hassan handed him the thermometer after having pretended, with carefully studied contortions, to pull it out of his anus. The orderly examined the thermometer, then stared suspiciously at the patient. Hassan had pulled the sheet up to his chin and closed his eyes so he wouldn't give himself away.

"Are you going to tell me where you put this thermometer?"

Hassan slowly opened his eyes.

"Where it's supposed to be put."

"And just where is that, where it's supposed to be put?"

The tone was rude, even threatening.

"So, here in front of me, you put it where it's supposed to go. Watch out, kid! Here you aren't home with your mother. With Ali Benkriou, no joking around. When I bring you the thermometer, put it in your ass and not under your balls. They've tried that one on me. Be careful, kid."

Titine was humming a tune as she came in with the breakfast cart. As Hassan's room was at the very end of the corridor, she sat on the bed and asked the new patient several questions to satisfy her curiosity.

"What's your name?"

"Hassan."

"Mine's Titine. Call me Titine. Isn't it pretty?"

She began to laugh.

"Drink your coffee. It'll get cold. You go to school?"

"Yes, to the *lycée*."

"Oh, the *lycée*! My father had his diploma. His *lycée* diploma! Next week I'll bring you a pair of pants."

"I have a pair of pants, Madame."

"No matter. That'll make you one more. I have a houseful that my children don't wear any more now that they're grown up. I'll pick out a nice pair for you."

"I don't need pants, Madame."

"Call me Titine. See you later. I have work to do in the kitchen."

"I swear I don't need pants, Madame."

Titine walked off singing, weightless behind her cart as if gliding on an invisible cloud.

The other bed in the room was soon occupied by a boy Hassan's age brought in as an emergency case one evening. He had had one eye put out by an arrow during a game of cowboys and Indians in a suburb of Boufarik.

"I was cut off from my friends. The Indian was hiding behind a tree, and I didn't see him."

Hassan put his things away for him, gave him the bedpan and the basin, but when the cowboy invited him, in the most natural way, to wipe his behind clean with a sheet of paper, he pulled back. Such a lack of manners left him trembling. Never, but never, would he have asked such a thing of another person.

The cowboy's mother was even more startling: she wore a veil, traveled alone by bus and spoke French with the nurses.

She was the sort of woman Hassan had never met in his village. She would bring little savory dishes in a straw basket covered by a napkin, dishes that she divided between her son and Hassan. She didn't stay long; the schedule for the bus had been moved up because the road was no longer safe.

"May God cure you, my son! Get well quickly so you can come home. Every day there are dead in this city. And you as well, my child, may God send you back to your family with your eyes!"

Saïd did not like chairs. He sat down cross-legged at the base of the wall and spoke loudly using peasant expressions. It was the colonist's dog where his father worked that had bitten him in the face, tearing away part of an eyelid.

"So, Hassan! What's in the papers? You understand French so well."

"It said: 'The war is over, it's a cease-fire.'"

Saïd shook his head as if to say, "It isn't true!" Then, without transition, he spoke of Titine's thoughtfulness and the nice pants she had brought him. He found them a bit long, but that didn't matter. When he got home, his mother would fix them for him.

"If you want, I'll give you mine too," proposed Hassan.

"And mine too," added the cowboy.

Saïd was delighted. That made three pants for him that were almost new. He would give one pair to his brother.

"So? What the paper says, is that true? Do you think the war is really over?"

He glanced toward the door, and then he took a white metal

tobacco container out of his pocket. He drew out a big wad and luxuriated in wedging it between his tongue and lower jaw.

"What I don't understand in this eye hospital," he said, as if talking to himself, "is the eyes they take out just like that. God protect me! They didn't take my eye out. Yours either, Hassan. But your friend, poor guy, he only has one eye. And in my room, there's Nigrou. He only has one eye left. But he doesn't really care. He slept under trucks. He doesn't have a home. Somebody came one night and hit him in the eye with a club. Poor Nigrou! And in the room next to yours, there's the guy from Indochina. He only has one eye too. You heard him: 'My eye! My eye! Oh, my head! Where is my eye?' The nurse told him, 'Your eye's in a bottle.' And after that, he didn't cry any more. And the fellow from Bouïra, they took out one of his eyes, too. But he doesn't say a word. He just sighs, with his hand over the empty socket. He says a boy twelve years old threw a stone at him, right in the eye, because he and a friend's father had an argument. But he has seven brothers. He says it won't just happen like that. Listen, brother Hassan, you'll come with me tomorrow. We'll take a walk outside. I'll take you by the insane asylum. It's not far, right behind us. You can hear the crazy people screaming. It's scary. My uncle, my father's brother, went crazy. He didn't scream. He sang at night as he walked along the road. And when the soldiers came to the village, my father tied up his hands and feet with a rope so he couldn't go out. And he tied a scarf over his mouth. One day, my uncle broke the rope with his own hands and went out singing into the night, and the soldiers shot him. . . . Nigrou says that there's a doctor who eats the eyes of the people who come to him for help. Do you believe such a thing?"

Without changing position, Saïd spoke eloquently and chewed his tobacco until the nightwatchman showed up. Then he politely said goodnight and went to his own room.

. . .

The radio belonged to a merchant from Algiers, a fat man impressed with his own importance who had been hospitalized in the hope of reducing a tic that, to his great confusion, caused his eyes to blink frantically as soon as he sat down at the table. In order to avoid blushing in front of his mother, his sister, and his wife, he even ate his meals alone or with his eyes hidden behind black glasses. One day in a restaurant, an unknown man seated across from him had taken this signal in the wrong way and hurriedly changed his seat.

The merchant refused to touch the hospital food because it was too tasteless for him. He divided his portion among his neighbors, keeping only the dessert for himself. His mother, his sister, and his wife, completely veiled in white and very perfumed, came to see him on afternoons. They would kiss him respectfully on his shoulder and place on his night table at least two Algerian dishes whose aroma, a mixture of garlic, pepper, cumin, cinnamon, allspice, and bay leaf, had the other patients sniffing and salivating. He sat on his chair, torso erect, well separated from his neighbors by his row of visitors; he always ate with gusto and breathed sighs of comfort. At the end he wiped his mouth with a striped napkin, thanking the Lord of

Heaven and Earth in a loud voice for His blessings and bound-less mercy. The women put back the empty utensils in the bas-ket, once more brushed the shoulder of the beloved patient with their delicate lips, wished all the others quick recovery in a kind of off-stage whisper, and went on their way.

"Independence, my children, is something very beautiful," said the merchant sunk into a pillow embroidered in silk that his wife had brought him despite hospital rules against it.

A cavernous cough shook Nigrou so strongly that it cut short his breath.

"You, Nigrou, today you live in the street. You're a drifter. Well, tomorrow when there's Independence, you will have a house with running water, electricity, an inside toilet, and you can marry and have children."

"I want a palace or nothing," said Nigrou very seriously.

"If such is your wish, we will fulfill it," said the merchant, without losing his calm. "Palaces will be built in abundance, with marble, gold, and fountains. And there will be gardens, orchards, flocks, and minarets will be as numerous as stars in the sky. Everything will be the way it once was. It will be like paradise. Every man on this earth will see his wishes come true. If you want a field, you'll have a field; if you want a horse, you'll have a horse; if you want a store, you'll have a store; if you want an automobile, you'll have an automobile."

"I want a palace," said Nigrou.

"I want a bicycle," said Saïd.

"Peace is enough for me," said an old farmer from Chélif smiling to himself as he listened to the merchant.

"For me, when Independence comes, I'll go to Mecca," said Amar, the policeman for the floor, in a dreamy voice as he stood leaning against the doorframe.

"France forbade us a lot of things, but never touched the pilgrimages. I've been to Mecca three times, and it's wonderful to go to Mecca."

"They say that Mecca pigeons do their crapping all over the houses of the city, but never on the venerable Kaaba."

"They don't crap on the House of God. God's House is pure."

"So you're saying that the pigeons of Mecca know that the Kaaba is the House of God?"

"Don't blaspheme, children. God has the power to inspire His creatures."

"I always dreamed about going to Mecca. I want to cleanse my bones: I sinned a lot when I was young."

"Who can boast he did not sin in his youth? Youth is the time for sinning. God is kind and merciful."

"I sinned a great deal," Amar went on, sounding like a public confession.

"We have all sinned."

The merchant closed his eyes.

The family oasis, his father's palm grove. He was wearing a robe festooned with silk, with a low-cut neck, all of the same color, blue. He was lighter-skinned than the other children—his mother was from the North—cleaner, and his hair was straight. The Koranic teacher had him sit next to him. He never struck him or scolded him. At the end of class he would keep him on, caressing him with a trembling hand and murmuring strange words. Sometimes, he would take him on his knees and put his arms around him. He would moan, breathe heavily, and not loosen his grasp until he had exhaled a great humid sigh against the child's neck. Then he would go to the back of the room and signal to the child with his hand that he should leave. The child would feel troubled when he got home, but he said nothing to anyone about the teacher's actions. When the teacher came to his father's store, either to buy things or to collect his fee, he would flatter the child publicly and place his hand on the boy's head. The child did not have the courage to look him in the face. He remained paralyzed, eyes lowered. His father would shake him by the arm.

"What are you waiting for to kiss your teacher's forehead!"

One afternoon, just before getting back to school, three boys Hassan's age barred his way and called him by a girl's name.

"What do you want with me?"

"To shaft you the way the teacher does."

The words struck him like a thunder clap, and he jumped back. His face was on fire, and then his whole body. He threw himself on one of the boys, grabbing him by the neck with both hands, and shook him so furiously that he fell to the ground. The two others fled. Without loosening his vise, he hammered at the boy's body with his knees until the boy's eyes, filled with terror, began to flutter. A passerby came running over and succeeded in making him let go. Hassan did not go to school. He went out into the palm trees, walking aimlessly till evening, hands tight-fisted. The next day, he gave a bad recitation of the

Koran, breaking one by one the verses and distorting the multiple attributes of Allah with an air of defiance. The teacher congratulated him on a good recitation, but when they were alone together after the other students had left, he said to him:

"What is the matter, my child? Tonight, you gave a bad recitation."

"I did it on purpose," the student dryly replied.

"That is not good. You should not do such things. It is a sin to distort the Koran."

"I don't care."

The teacher stretched out his hand to caress him. The child drew back, face closed and hard.

"If you touch me again, I'll tell everything to my father!"

His frail voice was trembling. That phrase had been running around in his head and burning in his throat since the night before. But now that he had thrown it into the teeth of the teacher, he was afraid. He backed up against the wall, and at that very instant, something changed in him. A ferocious willpower, whose nature he did not yet comprehend, began forming inside him. The teacher was already standing over him, cane in hand, crimson with indignation, massive, vociferating.

"Scorpion! What are you daring to insinuate? Get out of my sight or I'll break every bone in your body!"

The child went home feeling happy. Thoughts, ill-defined images that he perceived as imperative and crazy, bubbled inside him.

The child spoke to no one of his adventure. In the months that followed, he applied himself to the study of the Koran and neglected no effort to please the teacher. He became the intimate friend of the teacher's son, who was his own age and whom he showered with delicacies: dates, sugar-coated almonds, biscuits brought daily in his pockets from his father's grocery. The child had changed his blue smock for baggy trousers with black and white stripes, and a vest with copper buttons. He was tall and slender, and more and more handsome. At siesta time, the two children would go out under the palm trees, away from prying eyes, and would divide up the delicacies with smiles of complicity. The teacher's son had gentle eyes, and curly hair so tangled it looked as though he had run through the wind. The child would stretch out on top of him, and his sex, moistened with saliva, would slip into his anus.

The child had become a regular visitor at the teacher's house. The teacher's wife greatly admired him for his courtesy and his good looks. He always brought something with him, bread with sesame seeds with a golden crust that his mother had baked, eggs, a little basket of fruit. He even spent the night at the teacher's house, sleeping on shared matting and under a shared coverlet.

The wife had a tattoo on her forehead, a crown of blue leaves. Her eyes were black and shiny. The child would tremble with desire every time she placed her fleshy hot lips on his cheeks to wish him welcome. She would offer him a cup of coffee, and sometimes they were alone. Her eyes would seem even more shining. She teased him.

"You're a man now. Your mother is surely looking for a girl for you."

She would take him by the wrist and squeeze it to size up

his vigor and his virility. He could feel his sex get hard.

The child was in his fifteenth year when he finished his studies of the Koran. He had the sixty chapters of the Book at his fingertips. He recited them with the proper tone and rhythm, without a single false note. The teacher was proud of him. To celebrate the event, the father organized a ceremony at their home, with the teacher as guest of honor. After the meal, the child and the master, both dressed in white robes festooned with silk—a gift from the father—recited, in perfect harmony, the seven final chapters of the Koran. At midnight, the child kissed his teacher's forehead and accompanied him to his house. The teacher spoke of God; the child drank in his words.

The next day, the child took the wife a dress cut in the new fabric called "sea wave." It was a gift of honor chosen by his mother. The wife was alone in the house. She went into the next room to try on the dress. After a moment, she called the child. She was in her new dress, stretched out on a mat, thighs apart and sex awaiting. He penetrated her with a painful impetuosity. Eyes closed, the woman moaned and blessed him.

One autumn morning, the Koranic teacher did not wake up. The neighbors came running. He was dead, and no one knew why. Just the night before, he had recited seven chapters of the Book in a duet with the child. Aided by an elder of the village, the child dug the grave. The sun was already high, and the iron of the pickax struck harshly against the earth hardened by summer. When the elderly man went back to the village to get the body, the child lay down at the base of the grave, eyes closed. The freshness of the earth ran through his exhausted limbs and filled him with a sensual kind of pleasure.

At dusk he went back to the cemetery where nothing stirred. The fervor of the day had quieted down. He walked ahead like a sleepwalker, paying no attention to where he placed his feet. He trod on graves that were barely visible between the pebbles and dry bushes. He went over to the new grave with its stones piled up and slowly undid his fly.

The child walked among the dunes, staggering. His sex hurt him, in his body and in his mind. The pain rose from the earth, entering him, expanding and incandescent like a whirlwind of startled wasps. He wanted to run, but night lay heavily upon him and threatened to plunge him into the ground.

At dawn he sat down on a rock at the edge of a pond at the intersection of two irrigation ditches. Now there was a great silence in his body. Around him the universe seemed different. He looked at the light that came to rest on the palm trees, on his face, on his hands, on the water that flowed at his feet. The water was flowing and brought serenity and beauty to everything. He knelt down beside the irrigation ditch and, cupping his hands, splashed water on his face, then turned toward the east, eyes downcast. When he reopened his eyes, the sky, the earth, the trees, even the stones had disappeared. Only the water continued to murmur by his side. He stretched out his hand, ran it along the edge of the ditch and caressed the water.

The merchant from Algiers opened his eyes gently.
"Lord! Your mercy!"

Amar and the patients, still in their places, were deep in meditative silence. Hassan felt upset. He did not know whether the policeman on duty or the merchant from Algiers had just told the story, a sacrilege from one end to the other. Maybe no one had admitted any such thing. Could it not have been his very self, while the others were talking, who had invented all of that, pulling together scraps of conversation here and there, plus secretly guarded memories and desires turning in a void!

Days and nights were marked by the salvos of automatic weapons and the shrieking of ambulance sirens. The Delta Commandos, shaking with murderous madness, had been let loose. They were firing from the rooftops onto the Arab quarters. Trucks full of workers on their way back from work were being machine-gunned. Children still playing on the sidewalks were being shot point-blank. People were being tortured in cellars and their bodies tossed into the gutters. Post offices were sacked. Public buildings were set on fire.

Bit by bit, the hospital emptied. The cowboy, following his mother's advice, chose a glass eye and left. Saïd, Nigrou, the Algiers merchant, and many others who hadn't fully recovered preferred to go home. People felt safer at home, in their neighborhood, in their village, with their relatives, than in this hospital open to every breeze and buzzing with French employees who were closer to the OAS than to the Pro-Independence FLN. Arab employees became fewer and fewer. Hassan, who could see better at that time, helped Titine in the kitchen and the dining room.

She rewarded him with well-filled plates and double desserts.

His eye protected by a light bandage, Hassan wandered alone through the hospital corridors, stretched out on the empty beds or the marble floor of the waiting room, talked with the Indochinese nurse who assured continued treatments, and enjoyed himself going up and down in the elevator. Sometimes he went into the deserted operating area and lay down on the operating cart.

He had had only a local anesthetic, and he cried during the whole operation. He called for his mother, his father, implored God and the doctor, but nothing shortened his suffering. The doctors and their assistants quietly discussed things in front of him: the last bombs, the stores being closed, Kairouan mosque ready to explode, the White House teeming with people, Pompidou, Black-Rock, the condemnation of General Jouhand, the hanging of Eichmann and the throwing of his ashes into the sea. . . . And Hassan alone at the heart of his pain, crucified by the head to a tree of iron, naked before the rejected pity of the world. The moment came to take out the nail. Bloodless, conscience turns in on itself, coils about in a comforting torture as in the moments of lassitude and silence which used to follow the terrible punishments of his father. The carpet moves, takes flight, gently descends accompanied by a mysterious woman's voice that falls on the wound like a balm, a friendly shower: "We met, we recognized each other, we lost sight of each other, lost sight again, found each other, separated, then warmed up again, each on his own going off into life's whirl. . . . "

. . .

Cathy arrived in the afternoon, her dark hair spilling over her shoulders. She was Hassan's age. Her school, which she disliked, was closed. Her father, an important hospital administrator, had a villa next to the ophthalmological service. The girl went right into Maurice's room, Maurice a student non-com officer from Martinique. Hassan followed her in spite of himself, quietly went up to the door of the room and then, depressed, slowly left. The girl found him on the steps. She sat down facing him on a cement cornice, her back against a pillar, knees straight and apart. She openly stroked her thighs. He imagined or glimpsed her white panties, and his agitation increased. She laughed. She was happy. She didn't give a hoot about anything: soon she would be leaving for France with her parents.

The room next to Hassan's was occupied by an Algerian and a Frenchman who passed their time smoking and talking politics. Their discussions often grew bitter. They got heated, voices became shrill, and they overtly insulted each other.

"You're going to take over everything we've done. We're the ones who made this country into something. It's my father who made it. And now you're going to take it all away from us. You hear me, you're the winner and I'm the dupe."

"What could I take of yours? I'm as much a dupe as you are, a simple small restaurant owner. You know that very well."

"I don't know if you really are a restaurant owner, but I

know you're an Arab. It's written all over you. I even wonder if you're not a *fellaga* like the rest. And to think you're going to take everything from us: our beautiful houses, our cars, our gardens, and my bakery shop."

"And your sister!"

"Everything will end up in Arab hands. You're from Marengo. So you know Mitidja. Well, do you know what Mitidja was before we came? I'll tell you: a nest of mosquitoes and snakes. There are professors who wrote history books. Just see what Mitidja is like today: a bride in her veil! And to think that all that goes back to the Arabs!"

"The Arabs say shit to you! Enough! If you had been more fair. . . ."

"Oh yes, my dear sir! I was fair. I never stole from anyone, not even the Arabs. I've worked hard, and I pay my Arab workers well."

"You know why I've got an eatery? You know why I spend my days grilling bits of meat and my fingers too? Because France would have none of me in its administration! Even though I've got my diploma! I don't have it any more—I tore it up since they wouldn't have me. I swear I have my diploma."

Hassan expected them to resort to blows at any moment, but they would calm down and their conversation would become friendly again. The Algerian restaurant owner and the French baker ended up finding a point of agreement in the recognition of their powerlessness in the face of the mysterious forces of history that passed them by and fashioned their destiny.

. . .

Two bombs went off one morning within a couple of minutes of each other up in the important radiological service section of the hospital. The patients who still remained there—either because no one had come to get them or because their medical condition prevented their leaving the hospital—were badly frightened. "After the machines, it'll be the patients' turn. They're murderers; they're crazy; they spare no one. They even shoot children playing in the street." The hospital had no surveillance. People could enter at will.

At ten o'clock, several buses pulled into the hospital courtyard, escorted by unarmed militants of the FLN. They had the patients climb aboard and quickly piled the roof with dozens of mattresses, stacks of sheets and blankets thrown directly from the upper floors. Hassan had confidence in these men. Nevertheless, he didn't know where they were going. The buses moved in close convoy through the deserted streets. His companion, the restaurant owner from Marengo, pointed out places to him.

Past the Maison-Carrée, the Cité, the Mountain. The first two buses drove into the enclosure of a prefabricated trade school. A group of girls decked out in the Algerian colors—green, white and red—gave the patients an ovation as they helped them get off the bus before distributing them among the classrooms now converted into dormitories. A man in a white blouse asked Hassan how old he was, thought a moment, then walked toward the children's room. The mattresses were lined up side by side on top of blankets spread out on the floor. A center aisle with a solid wood table flanked by two benches separated the sexes.

At noon while the children were eating, two men came in. The first one, in a black suit and wearing sunglasses, was smoking a cigar. The second, in jeans and a checkered shirt, had a shiny machine gun across his breast. The man in the sunglasses looked at the nurse sitting at the end of the table, dramatically blew out a puff of smoke and said, "You children here need have no fear. Nothing's going to happen to you. Here you're in independent Algeria. We'll take care of you. . . . "

"Those dogs of the OAS are through," cut in the man with the machine gun. "Just let 'em come here!"

He tapped on the barrel of his gun.

"We have defeated France," continued the man with the glasses, stressing every syllable.

His annoyance was visible: he was the head of the center and couldn't stand to be interrupted. He inhaled ostentatiously on his cigar and added, "Our country is free now. We have many Algerian doctors, and they're the ones who are going to take care of you. And you're all going to get well."

"Am I going to get well too, Uncle?" asked a boy sitting in a wheelchair next to the nurse.

The man with the machine gun didn't leave his well-dressed companion the time to answer. "How did you become paralyzed like that?"

"I don't know. I was very little. A doctor gave me a shot and I haven't walked since."

"What's the doctor's name?"

"I don't know. I was in Bône."

"It was surely a Frenchman."

"Yes, it was a Frenchman."

"When you get well and are grown up, we'll send you to find him, and he'll be judged for his misdeeds the way the Jews did to Eichmann."

"So, Uncle, I'll get well!"

"Everybody will get well in independent Algeria. In independent Algeria, everybody will be well. When you have such a beautiful flag, you don't get sick."

The man with the glasses couldn't hide his impatience. Frowning, he left the room.

"Uncle, can I touch your machine gun?"

At a single stroke the man closed the clip and held the arm out to the boy who slid his hands along the butt and the barrel. The nurse smiled. The other children watched with envy and astonishment.

Hassan spent his days in the adult section equipped with small metal beds, clothes trees and chairs that replaced night tables. The hours went by in chitchat between the patients who had no care and nurses with no work due to a lack of medical prescriptions and medicine. One of the patients, who had a sprained ankle, was a former inmate of the El Harrach penitentiary. He fascinated Hassan with his accent, his tall tales, and his raw language that frightened the nurses. Sentenced to twenty years in prison, he had taken advantage of the general anarchy due to the cease-fire to escape by climbing over a wall. Without papers or family and with a painful foot, he had been taken in by FLN militants. They promised him a plane ticket to go home to his people in Casablanca as soon as the political situation was clarified.

"Don't listen, little one," said the restaurant owner from Marengo to Hassan. "I know people like him. He says he was put in prison for killing a Frenchman and that he was denounced to the police by a collaborator with the French. Now that the war is over, every convict on earth and every good-for-nothing is suddenly a militant nationalist. And everybody says, 'I killed a Frenchman, I killed a collaborator, I'm a member of the FLN, a revolutionary. . . . ' "

Hassan only went to the children's section for his meals and to sleep. Evenings the nurses gathered around the table and chatted, drinking Coca-Cola, their ears glued to a transistor. When a patriotic song came on, they stopped talking, listened, and then took up their conversation where they had left off.

"I'm going to save money and buy myself a car."

"A car! Are you sick in the head? What will your parents say?"

"I don't care. If they don't like it, I'll go live by myself. I've got work."

"If I did that, my father and brothers would cut my throat."

"What are you saying? Things aren't going to be the way they were. Things are going to change."

"What I'd like to do is to go to France, to travel. . . . "

"Well, I'm going to do both—buy a car and drive around France."

"Aren't you going to get married?"

"Oh no! I don't want to get married."

"Listen sister, you aren't normal. I'd say independence has driven you out of your wits. You're going to end up in trouble. You want to have it all!"

"So why else have we been at war for seven years?"

"Certainly not so women could go crazy and get ideas like you. . . . "

The children pretended to be asleep for they had been told it was time to go to sleep. They could have Coca-Cola the next morning with the midday meal. Men often came to see the girls, and late at night stifled laughter could be heard behind the shutters. Sometimes there would be a vague noise near the doorway where the night nurse had her bed. The next morning, the children would exchange secrets. At noon they would drink Coca-Cola and hum patriotic songs along with the nurses.

On the afternoon of July 2, there was an explosion of joy: salvos of firearms, ululating, dancing, tears, cries, embraces in the shadow of the green, white and red flag flying high over the rooftops. The result of the referendum was without appeal and Algeria was officially independent. The festive mood went on well into the night, led by the dancing Moroccan waving his hands over his head and singing prison songs in a loud voice. At dawn a violent dispute broke out in the courtyard, one that woke up the patients.

"I'm the boss here!"

"The boss is the one with the machine gun, and I'm the one with the machine gun. And just remember that all I have to do is pull the trigger and I shoot you down like a dog."

"You're the dog! When I was fighting the Revolution, you were pimping on the streets of Algiers. I'll have you locked up in Barberousse to teach you respect for revolutionaries."

"You shut up! Shut up! If this isn't a disgrace! Our country is barely independent and you're already devouring one another.

What next? What will things be like? Enough, you're bothering the patients."

The next morning, a bony-looking representative of the FLN with traces of burns on his face came to the center, along with four armed soldiers. He disarmed the man with the machine gun in front of everyone and pushed him toward the door shouting, "Algeria is independent since yesterday, and you're turning it into a bordello already. Out you go! On your way!"

He gave him a sound kick in the butt and slammed the door behind him. Then he turned to the nurses who had gathered there in the yard, and his eyes were shining.

"And you! Pack your bags right away. If you think independence means debauchery, you're wrong. Out you go!"

One of the girls began to sob. She fell in a faint into the arms of a companion. They stretched her out on a bed and sprinkled her forehead with cologne. She opened her eyes and saw the man who had just insulted her standing at the foot of the bed. She turned her head and started to cry again. The man shrugged his shoulders and left.

Outside the celebration was in full swing. Cars full of people, draped with flags, streaked through the streets, giving the liberty salute of five short honks, endlessly repeated to the rhythms of fist pounding on metal and of ululating. Both sexes mingled in the streets. As if by enchantment, everyone became brother and sister. Caught in the whirl of freedom and desire, the girls shed their veils, their modesty, and their fears, as they sat on the boys' knees and allowed themselves to be led off into the vineyards abandoned by the French colonists. As in fairy tales, the celebration went on for several days and nights. Strange rumors began to circulate. People said that in Algiers virgins had become so rare that there was talk of taking exceptional measures so as not to leave any deflowered girl without a husband—the first decisions by the new authorities. As the number of deflowered girls was so unusually large compared to the number of available men, each "male" would be obliged to take charge of two to four "females." So as not to offend anyone in the parcelling out of spouses, there would be a lottery. The women's names would be inscribed on pieces of cardboard that would be mixed up in a big potato sack.

At one end of the yard in the shade of an ash tree, the former prisoner was musing out loud. He was stretched out on his back, his head against a beam. Hassan, his back against the tree trunk, was listening.

"If the government wants to grant me a pension for every woman, I'm ready to take on a dozen. I'll do our Prophet one better, prayer and health be upon Him. And then it really will be like in paradise: eternal ecstasy."

He sat up on his elbow, took the last puff on his cigarette butt and added, in a voice that Hassan did not recognize, "What the boss said the other day is right. Now that this country is free, it shouldn't become a national bordello."

On July 10 the patients were taken back to the newly reopened hospital. Hassan and the restaurant owner from Marengo were alone in the ophthalmological section. But the next day they were joined by several other patients. Titine did not reappear. There was only one French doctor left and the Indochinese nurse, as affable and devoted as ever. Not all of the Algerian employees had come back either. Some got lost in the liberty celebrations; others, more devious and opportunistic, had left the hospital to slip off into positions of power in the new State: the police and their headquarters, the army, the party, and various administrative posts. The nurse Ali Benkriou was now installed in the office of chief administrator. He had named himself to this post, believing that the responsibility was his by right. So many factors militated in favor of this self-promotion: his age, his service record, his arrest by the French, and more important still, the return of his son from the underground wearing an officer's uniform. In order to assure his authority over his former colleagues, he had his son come by one afternoon, and strolled at length with him up and down the corridors without saying a word to anyone.

"He's a lieutenant."

"He's a captain, I tell you. Maybe even a major."

"He arrived in a jeep, three soldiers with him."

"Did you see his machine gun? That's what they call a Chinese machine gun. Capable of cutting down a hundred people a minute."

This visit proved to be very profitable because when the members of the staff began to dispute the doctors' white coats a week later on—the blue ones looked like uniforms for subordinates, and from now on unfit for free men's status—Benkriou put them firmly in their place. Methodical and concerned with justice, he drew up a list and set up a rotation for the distributing of the prestigious white coats.

Hassan's roommate, a young man of some twenty years from Tizi-Ouzou who came with an eye oozing blood, wore a military cap he said had been given to him by a leader of the Resistance. As soon as he awakened, he would adjust his cap and seat himself at the window by the women's wing while whistling the national anthem or a popular French song. He said he had been an unparalleled revolutionary fighter and every day he told Hassan, in great detail, a new episode of the heroic actions he had carried out in the Kabylie Mountains: time bombs set in many French bars and even in front of police headquarters, a military roadblock to take over the wheel of a DS-19, a chase zigzagging along the roads of Djurdjura, tires screeching and guns crackling. He spoke in a loud voice, his left foot on the chair, arms crossed on his chest. Hassan had the impression he was acting in a movie. He was reliving film sequences of cowboys, gangsters, war episodes, in this display of bravery. "Just call me Eddie Constantine because, you know, Eddie Constantine is just like me," he told Hassan one day.

One morning, Eddie Constantine woke up seething with anger. He slammed his fist down on the metal table.

"That's enough!"

Hassan turned around dumbfounded.

"I haven't done anything to you," he spluttered.

"I said: that's enough! I've been here ten days now, and the doctor's examined me only once. It's the fault of that bitch of a nurse. She didn't speak for me. She'll see who she's dealing with!"

He slapped his cap on his head and looking angry went out into the hallway. Suddenly there were sounds of cries and a door slamming. Then running in the hallway. The patients hurried out of their rooms. Eddie Constantine, holding on to the handle of the infirmary door and pulling violently on it, was yelling.

"The bitch! I'll kill her! I'll break down the door. Let her get the hell out to France!"

The employees succeeded in pushing the young hothead into the refectory, and the chief, now present, threatened to throw him out if he didn't quiet down. The nurse was seated on a chair crying inconsolably. The patients were upset and shocked. They were afraid the nurse would leave. They used words like crazy and imbecile for the pseudorevolutionary, now calmed down, sitting quietly in the empty dining room, head in hands, facing the cap now lying on the table.

When the afternoon ended and the nurse got off from work, Hassan was sitting on the pavilion steps. The nurse shook his hand.

"Goodbye, Hassan."

There were almost tears in her voice. Hassan felt touched and upset. He had the feeling of something irreparable. She had never bid goodbye that way before. Usually she called him from a distance or gave him a little tap on the shoulder when she went by him. The red silhouette moved into the distance. Hassan wished he could hold on to her in his mind's eye, but she was already too far away, almost out of range of his weakened eyesight. She was nothing more than a red spot, a drop of blood, an incandescent point implanted in memory. Hassan felt immense fatigue take over his body. He returned to his room, stretched out on his bed and turned his face to the wall.

Four ex-Resistance fighters were among the patients. Three of them, almost blind, had come with their weapons, revolvers that they kept under their pillow. The other patients, civilians, gathered around them, curious and flattered to really get to know true Resistance fighters wounded in combat. They showed them every consideration, acted as guides for them, as errand boys or simply as attentive listeners. Like all the rest, Hassan spent hours listening to them, seated on the tile floor or on a chair. The narration of their life as fighters, punctuated with violence, blood, and death, had all the fascination of a fairy tale. They evoked some of the vicissitudes of the long nightmare from which Algeria was just emerging, a nightmare whose horror anyone not having been burnt in the blaze could hardly imagine.

"It was just one week after the declaration of the ceasefire. I said, 'I haven't seen my uncle for a long time. Now I don't risk anything by going to visit him.' We ate well. It did me good. I hadn't eaten that well for months. We talked for a long time. During the night, my cousin came into the room where I was sleeping. She was eighteen, bright as the sun. I showed my her machine gun. I said, 'I'm still married to the other one. Be patient, cousin!' I left at dawn. The family was still asleep. The road was dark. They were hidden behind the bushes. Who told them I was there? They knocked me to the ground. There were three of them. They loaded me into a tarpaulin-covered truck, gagged me, tied me, and left me half dead. It was still night. People were still asleep. They put me in a huge cellar. There was a very big man behind a desk. What was his name? He said his name. I don't remember it. 'Take a good look.' He stuck a photo under my nose. 'No, I don't know him.' 'It's a friend of yours, a *fellaga* like you. He works at the fishery. You think you've won. Take a good look: today is his last day on earth.' He worked up a mouthful of sputum that he spat into my face. The others burst out laughing. Next thing I was in the toilets. With a blowtorch, they branded a star on my back. You can see it if you like. A star of fire in my back. I fell down into a toilet hole and I could feel them urinating on me. He put the barrel of a revolver to my temple. When I came to, I was in a hospital, my head wrapped in bandages, my eyes empty. The ambulance drivers had picked me up a week earlier in the gutters of Algiers. They thought I was dead."

"That time, the mission was shaping up into something even more dangerous. The men of Messali were always on their guard, and they knew how to fight, real snakes. We were supposed to use only knives. It's hard to escape the Paris police. I was the one who was supposed to kill the pig. The two others went to help me subdue him. A colossus, a tough guy. We broke in the door, and had a lot of trouble subduing him. And there he was sobbing and begging for mercy. 'I'm an Algerian like you. I'm your brother. I swear I'll pay up, I'll work with you.' I said, 'Nothing to be afraid of, brother. We aren't going to harm you. But we have to undress you and tie you to your bed so we can tell the chief when we get back that we undressed you and tied you to the bed. That's all the punishment we decided for you. Just cooperate and it'll be all right.' He took off his clothes himself. He easily let us tie him on his bed. I pulled out my knife. My companions were at the door. I started to walk around the bed and talk about the Cause, about the Revolution. My eyes were looking for the heartbeat on his hairy chest. I saw it. I stood still. I took a fix on the heart. I took a deep breath. I struck. He stiffened. I pulled out the blade. He slumped down with such force that he overturned the bed. A colossus, a tough guy. I struck again. And I struck again. And I struck again."

While people were celebrating Independence, whole battalions of the new Algerian army were confronting one another in a fratricidal struggle for power. Every time a military convoy or an important person went through a village, the inhabitants massed along the road, dancing and singing and shouting all the names that had meant hope to them in the terrible war years. Profiting from the political confusion, those who were clever settled their life's affairs; some used predated notarized documents to acquire buildings, movie houses, restaurants, stores, factories, and other possessions hastily abandoned by the former colonists; others, taking advantage of the role they said they had played secretly in the Revolution, replaced their former bosses at the head of an agricultural property or a commercial enterprise. In order to force the departure of those who lingered or refused to go and to take over their belongings as quickly as possible, there were attempts to terrorize them by throwing stones at their windows at night and shouting curses at them during the day. The most daring of the inhabitants of shantytowns attacked buildings that were under construction, forcing apartment doors and taking possession. Hadn't they been told that Independence would mean the end of their misery! Some who were looking for rougher entertainment with the smell of blood and others who wanted to have a revolutionary act inscribed on their record, even one after the event, organized themselves to hunt down collaborators.

III

August 10, 1962

Hassan's father was taking a nap stretched out on the counter of his grocery store, the tail end of his turban covering his eyes. The ambulance driver shook his shoulder.

"Wake up, Youssef. I'm bringing your son home."

Youssef lifted his turban and, seeing his son standing in the doorway, got up, his face bright with happiness. He gingerly slipped down from his perch and walked barefoot across the cement floor. The little store quickly filled with people. The café owner, the barber, a taxi driver, two or three grocers, some gawkers, and some children who stole quietly out of their dark corners made a circle around Hassan who was seated on an old packing box, his suitcase between his legs. They guilelessly asked about his eyes and about the results of the operation he had undergone. His father handed out peanuts to Hassan and the children crouched in front of the counter.

"And the newspaper print, can you read it?"

He held out a page of the paper he had taken from among some sheets beside the scales.

"I can see the road. I see human forms. I see colors too, but I still can't see newsprint. I can only see some black marks," said Hassan as he tried to hold back his emotions.

"You can't see the writing on the newspaper! Then you aren't cured yet."

The father's eyes filled with tears. He went to the back of the store. A big tear rolled down his nose and disappeared into his gray mustache. The taxi driver, who had seen everything, couldn't keep from crying either.

"Come along. I'm going to take you to your mother. She must be waiting for you, the poor thing."

The car went down the main street bathed in sunlight and silence. Hassan had the impression of driving through a phantom village, empty of any trace of life. Forewarned by a daughter who had been playing under a tree, his mother came running out of her house, face unveiled. She threw her arms around her son's neck, covering him with kisses as she asked him again and again how he was feeling. Once in the house, when she saw Hassan's hesitant movements, she understood that he had not recovered his normal sight. She began to cry.

"I told you very clearly, son, that your problem couldn't be taken care of by French medical doctors," she said through her tears. "I'll sell my jewelry, what little I have, I'll sell it all and, if need be, I'll go see all the seers and healers."

His father, seated on a bench, held his tongue. Hassan breathed with difficulty. His eyes filled with tears. He felt somewhat responsible for the pain he was causing his parents by coming back from Algiers with his eyes still afflicted. Malek, seated on the floor, was staring at this brother. Suddenly he got up on his little legs, his face lit up with joy.

"Mama! Mama! The rooster! The rooster! You really said, 'We'll cut its throat when Hassan comes back from Algiers.' I'll go get it."

He ran toward the door and leaped down the steps with his arms wide open.

"It's the rainbow-colored rooster. Remember? I kept it for your homecoming."

"He's fat as a calf," said Youssef who was already searching through his pocket for the pen knife lost in a fistful of coins and seeds destined for the garden.

When he woke up, Hassan saw his mother seated beside him sewing a talisman onto a square of old gazelle skin. She was looking at him with a smile, a bit embarrassed and a bit upset, silently begging for his understanding. She knew how capable he was of making fun of the old beliefs and the practices of the wise men.

"It came from Master Mokran's hand. I went at least five times to his house before I found him in. He was always out. I had to beg him, because he doesn't write out any more talismans. The third time, your father went with me in a taxi."

By mentioning the father who had never hidden his hostility toward the charlatans, she hoped she could ward off any impulse toward rebelliousness on her son's part. Hassan said nothing. The needle in his mother's fingers fascinated him. She pricked

the leather, supplely pierced it, made a curve, and then stuck in
the needle with the same precision. Neither haste nor fits and
starts. Her fingers barely moved. The motion was fluid. Just as
he liked to watch his mother weed out grain, he liked to watch
her sew. How tranquil she seemed to him at those moments. . . .

"If you don't want to wear it around your neck, at least put it
in your pocket. Master Mokran says you must always have it
with you. I'll attach a thread if you want to wear it around your
neck. But do as you wish, my son. If you want to get well. . . . "

"I'll put it in my pocket," Hassan heard himself say.

There was a submission in his voice that astonished him. A
sinuous stream of water ran through his mother's fingers.

Hassan as a child is lying in front of the fireplace, gravely
ill. Outside it is winter, silence. His mother, seated beside him,
shoulders wrapped in a blue shawl held to her breast by a silver
brooch, is sewing a talisman into a square of gazelle skin.
Hassan, eyes wide open, sees a slender stream of shining water
run continuously from his mother's fingers, traversing the
gazelle skin as it curves through space.

"It has been snowing since this morning. The sky is touch-
ing the earth," sighs Fatim-Zohra who begins a strange story
about what people say happened to a very sick man, one known
and respected by all.

Hassan closes his eyes. A wicker cradle on the end of a long
cord slowly descends from the sky. Far up above him in the
middle of the white sky, he hears the grating of a pulley.

116

"Are you sleeping, my son?"

Hassan opens his eyes and flutters his eyelids. He is happy to be with his mother again, with her tattoos, her shawl, and the water that runs from her fingers onto the talisman on the gazelle skin.

"When the man got to heaven, two angels welcomed him, the angel of death and his brother, the angel of life. He saw them. He heard them. The angel of death said: 'He has used up his days. Today he has reached his term of life.' The angel of life said: 'He is a man of good deeds, predestined to reside with the blessed. Let us grant him several more years.' The dispute between the two angels lasted a long time, one wanting to keep the man and the other to return him to his family. It's the angel of life who finally won out. The man was returned to earth on the end of a cord. When he opened his eyes, his wife and children were around him crying. He shook his head and said, 'My hour has not yet come.' "

Fatim-Zohra lost no time. Early that afternoon, she put on her veil and, followed by her two sons, started out for Mother Zibouda's house up above the village on the first foothills of the mountains. Hassan was carrying a basket stuffed with a long bread from the bakery and a branch of dates. Malek was squeezing a chicken attached by the feet and half asleep in his arms. Mother Zibouda had told Fatim-Zohra, who often went to consult her, to bring Hassan to her as soon as he came back from the hospital. She was capable not only of penetrating the mysteries of his illness, but also of restoring his sight.

When the young man who supervised the sainted woman's household took the visitors into a low-ceilinged room, Mother Zibouda was against the wall with her legs stretched out on a mat. Hairy, emaciated, and her yellow forehead intersected by an eagle's claw drawn in methylene blue, her eyes closed, she was holding a cigarette between her fingers. Several scarves of different colors rolled one on top of the other covered her head.

One afternoon, a police motorcycle went by on the road, spreading trouble. The women, opening their doors wide, were calling to one another, asking questions, and exchanging words of compassion. Something serious had happened in the houses up above near the mountain. A man named Ayach had shot his neighbor and then his own wife with a revolver. Then he tried to shoot his daughter, a baby a year old that an old neighbor woman had barely managed to save by carrying her away. The motorcycle went by again, followed by the truck of the commune with the two corpses side by side, wrapped in woolen blankets. Behind closed doors the women were reciting formulas to conjure away bad luck. That evening, in the houses the death truck had passed, the cooking pot was placed on the fire.

When he returned to the village after ten years in prison, Ayach took a woman's name and put on women's clothes and became known as a diviner, a healer, and an unraveller of evil spells. He quickly acquired a reputation among the women for saintliness. Some women venerated him and used his name on taking oaths, and what they all remembered when going to see him was the indispensable package of cigarettes.

"My daughters, don't bring me anything if you wish, but don't forget the package of cigarettes," he told his visitors.

Mother Zibouda rubbed her cigarette butt against the wall and sat up on one elbow. Fatim-Zohra shoved the chicken toward her and the open basket. Mother Zibouda put her hand in the basket, blindly felt the packages, then shuffled them around as if looking for something that should be there but that she could not find. Fatim-Zohra gave a malicious smile.

"It isn't in the basket, Mother. I was afraid it would get crushed."

She slipped her hand under her dress and pulled out a package of Bastos cigarettes. Then the saint sat up, legs coiled up under her dress. In a hoarse voice and panting, she told Hassan to come close. She contemplated him for some time, her hand on his shoulder.

"Look straight at me. I'm in front of you. Can you see me?"

"I can see you, but there's a kind of mist in front of my eyes."

"Your eyes aren't looking straight ahead. They're turning to the left."

"Yes, Mother, he looks to one side ever since he got sick," said Fatim-Zohra.

"Yes, I understand. I see it. I already told you that, my daughter. Your child was hit by a *djinn*. He was slapped on the right cheek, and his eyes swung to the left. They could even have come all the way out of their sockets. God protected him."

Mother Zibouda had spoken in a barely audible voice. One might have thought she feared her revelations would be over-heard by some invisible being in her audience or on sentry duty in a corner of the room.

"We accept God's will, Mother," said Fatim-Zohra.

"Child, lie down on your left side."

Hassan obediently stretched out on the grass mat. The saint measured him three times from head to toe using the span of her hand. She recited verses from the Koran. Sensitive to tickling, Hassan felt like laughing. He controlled himself thinking what chagrin he would cause his mother, who was so convinced of the saintliness and the occult powers of the former convict. Mother Zibouda pulled down one of the many scarves over her eyes, coiled herself up in a ball, covered her face with her hands, and did not move. Fatim-Zohra anxiously held her breath. Whenever Mother Zibouda went into this kind of trance, she was in touch with the invisible world, speaking with the spirits and beseech-ing them to show her the path to follow for bringing relief to men in their suffering. Sometimes, when the spirits refused to answer her, she would begin to groan and utter moaning sounds that filled Hassan's mother with terror. She had even been seen to weep hot tears. She came out of her trance. Her body relaxed. She crossed her legs under her dress and lifted up the scarf that hid her eyes. Her lips moved. Fatim-Zohra leaned forward.

"You have to buy a young black goat. You have to cut its throat Thursday night. You have to cook it in a new cooking pot. You have to serve it on a large platter. You have to give it to the patient isolated in a dark room, door and windows closed. The *djinns* will come to partake of the meal and will take the illness with them when they leave. You have to throw the bones into the river at midnight."

Everything took place as the saint had recommended: the choice of the goat, the day of the sacrifice, the cooking pot that had never been used, the isolation of Hassan in a dark closed room with an enormous platter of boiled smoking meat in front of him. Hassan did not believe in *djinns*, but finding himself alone in the dark and silence faced with such a quantity of meat, for him who had never liked boiled meat, he felt panic-stricken. He vainly tried to get hold of himself. His childhood fears were already there, crowding around him, crouching in corners, hanging from the ceiling, or roosting on the coffer and the armoire, ready to crush him just as they were when his sister would shove him into a darkened room and lie down on his body while baring her horse-like teeth. He would struggle, yelling, and in the end would no longer be able to distinguish between the voracious mouth of his sister and the vague mass that was trying to suffocate him. His terror grew, his cries got louder until finally his sister loosened her hold and ran off neighing like a horse. Hassan, nausea on his very lips, fearfully seized a morsel, raised it to his mouth and threw it back immediately. He gave the platter a kick with his heel that sent it smashing into the base of the armoire. He got to his feet, furious, and violently pushed open the door.

The atmosphere of the village had completely changed, going from one extreme to another as if in a fairy tale. Nevertheless, people didn't seem surprised, as though things could be only that way, the change having come unexpectedly like a benevolent act of fate etched into the very order of existence.

The barracks were now inhabited by Algerian soldiers. Strapped up tight in new leather, rifles shining on their shoulders, they would go to the stadium to learn to how march in step or up to the surrounding hills to practice shooting. Through the keyhole or the crack of a door, women waxed ecstatic over the fine figures cut by their men, and girls fantasized about themselves in glorious wedding ceremonies. The men confidently stopped to say hello, giving thanks to God for having delivered them from the oppressors. Looking triumphant in khaki shirts acquired in the unloading, they were escorted by the children and wore homemade, fancifully put together rifles slung over their shoulders, sometimes carrying real bullets in their pockets. In the afternoon when the soldiers would go strolling through the village, the children, curious, would surround them, calling them by name or by a nickname, and creating an uproar by yelling the name of one of the girls.

There were hardly any Frenchmen left in the village. They had departed during the first days of Independence: the realists, after having sold houses and furniture at any price to middle-class Algerians accustomed to the ways of bargaining; the utopians—those who believed they would return through the conviviality of communities—after turning the keys to their property over to someone they trusted. Doctor Aouiz, formerly a target of the FLN, was still at the hospital, intimidating both personnel and patients with his outbursts and legendary fits of anger. A delegation of important people, including even those underground fighters responsible for almost having killed him, paid him a visit one evening and pleaded with him—in the name of the finally reestablished brotherhood and harmony among peoples—not to leave for France, not to leave them without someone to care for them.

The leaders were feared and respected. To establish their authority, no sooner had they arrived in the village than they acted with severe cruelty in matters of morality. People still spoke in whispers about the true or imagined punishment inflicted on two villagers accused of adultery. The woman had her head shaved, and the man had his genitals burned with the point of a red-hot sickle. People also remembered the belligerence of the leaders in making those who had escaped the revolutionary contributions during the war years pay up. The baker, who saw no reason to pay war taxes in peacetime, was thrown into a ditch and trampled by a leader in a rage. Struck by such violence, the others, despite the amounts exacted and the rumors about where the money really went, paid up without any fuss.

As for the death of Zaïdi the café owner, it caused confusion and stupor among the villagers. He had collapsed on the floor of his own café, under the eyes of his son, a child of nine. A great number of people followed his coffin, their minds teeming with questions that had no answers. Perhaps the leaders weren't wholly in their right minds. Seven years of war and suffering was enough to make someone crazy. He hadn't wanted to kill his friend. It was just a game that turned out badly. He had wanted to simulate the gesture of death without killing, to have a laugh with the others sitting sipping the hot sweet-smelling coffee that Zaïdi had just served them. He said: "Zaïdi, I press on this and there's no more Zaïdi on earth." Zaïdi looked straight at his friend, no challenge, no fear, only a big question mark. Why this joke in bad taste? The others were laughing. "You see what your life depends on. I pull on this piece of iron and bye-bye Zaïdi." The shot went off. Everybody in the café froze—gestures, looks, voices, breathing, petrified. In the eyes of the café owner there was still the same question mark. He slowly slumped down, and his forehead knocked the coffee cup over on the table. He didn't want to kill his friend. It was Satan the evil one who pulled the trigger. An accident. God wished it! A former fighter, a former internee in the camps, Zaïdi was declared a martyr of the Revolution. A case-file was set up to give a pension to his widow and orphans, and the matter was closed.

Sycophants with calculating eyes, always willing to render service to their new friends, spring up around leaders. If the chief needs an automobile for his pleasure, one comes along at top speed. If the chief wants to get married, they loosen their purse strings to help with the purchase of furniture and sheep. On the marriage day, they lend their kitchen utensils, their tables, their chairs, their tablecloths, their rugs, and their wives and children to help with the service. In short, they spare themselves neither trouble, fortune, nor imagination in order to please their leaders.

One after another, the true and the false revolutionaries took wives. For these men, marriage to a well-educated beautiful girl from a rich family seemed like a rite of passage for returning to peacetime, for entering the garden of plenty and delight. Any other opinion seemed unworthy of their consideration. They fought, they suffered, they won, now they expected to live and enjoy without restrictions. What could be more legitimate! More than one chief, already married and a father, preferred to remarry in order to conform with this hedonistic morality.

Naturally the leaders occupied positions of power. As for the others, the simple underground fighters and militants, most of them uneducated, they were assigned the jobs of administrators' orderlies, of rural or city policemen, and night watchmen who had once served under the French but had been forced out, usurpers who were finally unmasked. The *chouhadas*, the martyrs, were not forgotten. Their families were cared for, their widows and parents were promised pensions. Their children were given customary circumcision ceremonies. Their heroic deaths were remembered. Their bones, dispersed throughout the country, were searched out so they could have a tomb worthy of their sacrifice in the cemetery of their native village with their name on the tombstone.

The cortege left early to avoid the scorching heat. Hassan and his brother Lahcen formed part of it. They had both learned their first Koranic verses under the direction of the indulgent Si Brahim. Hassan recalled his surprise, his questions, and his foreboding when, from one day to the other, he saw no more of his teacher. People said he was on a trip, first to Sétif, then to Bougie, without giving any explanations. One night, a shot rang out in the neighborhood. French soldiers arrived immediately, crossed the gardens, looked in the ravines, and searched houes without finding anything. Later on, Hassan learned that his Koranic teacher had left the guerrillas to go visit his family, for his wife had just given birth to a son. In spite of the risks he was taking, he had fired a shot to celebrate, this man who until then had only daughters. But one day, there was talk of his death over there toward the north in the ocher-white hills beyond the gully.

Didou was waiting underneath a tree, surrounded by his dogs. He joined the procession. The man carrying the hunting rifle, arm out authoritatively, stopped him.

"And the dogs, part of the procession?"

"They won't bother anyone. They walk on their own legs."

Three or four persons turned around, either through curiosity or to express their disapproval.

"You blaspheme all day long, and now you come with your dogs!"

"Dogs to go find our martyrs!"

"May Allah turn you to stone here and now!"

"I don't want to waste time on words. If they come with us, I will shoot them full of buckshot."

A smile shining from the bright, quick eyes danced over Didou's wrinkled face, a face divided between irony and pity. Not saying a word, Didou went back to the foot of the tree and sat down among his dogs. He spoke with them, then got to his feet and ran up to rejoin the procession. The dogs turned tail and went off down the road.

The procession crossed the stony bed of the gully. The musicians who were marching at the head of the column sounded the bagpipe and the tambourine. One man waved a flag on a stick, and the mother of Si Brahim waved a green scarf with red fringe from the end of her arm. The man with the rifle threw back his shoulders and fired a shot, starting up ululations. They were entering a village. Other ululations responded, coming out of the houses at the same time as the women and children who began to applaud as they jumped up and down and cried out,

"Long live our martyrs!" A farmer in his garden next to the road washed his hands in the stream and joined the procession. From a stone bench, a man busily planing down a branch of wood called out, "Brothers! Wait! You must be thirsty. I'll bring you some of this morning's milk."

"Thank you, brother! The road is long. We have to hurry to avoid getting burned by the sun," said the man with the rifle.

A white shadow detached itself from high on a chalk hill, the blue sky behind it. In the light, by now intense, and with the chirrings of insects that arose from the stubble of the fields, the figure seemed to move in ways that eluded any attempts by the eye to make out its contours. Two shots sounded. The white shape moved off, carried by the echo that traveled from one cliff to another. The silhouette of a horseman took shape bit by bit moving like a slow pendulum. It was Saïd, the "Lightning Bolt." He came down to meet the procession riding on a old white mare, his head covered by a white turban twisted with black cord and wearing a white *gandoura* with yellow silk embroidery around the low neckline, a wide-legged trouser cut at mid-calf, red stockings, one hand tight on the reins and the other holding a double-barrelled shotgun with an inlaid butt. The old man dismounted, and everyone hurried over to embrace him. He pulled the mare behind him, the procession following in line. Farther on, under a great lone hawthorn, his son Ali, looking almost as old as his father, was waiting. Beside him were a pickax, a shovel, a jug and, hanging from a branch, a wet goatskin. Lightning Bolt Saïd let go of the mare, hung his rifle from a branch, turned to the south, and walked straight ahead. He counted seventeen steps aloud.

"There. Right there," he said, as he stooped down.

He tapped the hardened earth with his palm.

"When the French soldiers came to get us, he was lying right there on his left side, knees curled up, hands on his stomach. He was sleeping. A child. His breast was red, and this earth also. Isn't that right, son?"

Ali, standing near him, imperceptibly nodded his head. Si Brahim's mother approached, her face bathed in tears. She sat down and picked up a handful of earth that she wrapped in a handkerchief. Saïd got up again, calculated the space once more and walked ahead. He counted ten paces and said, "We buried him here. It was my son Ali who dug the grave."

Hassan was waiting under the hawthorn tree. Suddenly a woman as wide as she was tall, the only one who kept on her veil despite the heat, bent over him as if she had just become aware of his presence and began to kiss him effusively on both cheeks.

"Your mother told me you spent a lot of time in Algiers. Didn't you hear any mention around you of the sheik?"

It was the second wife of Si Bachir, the father of Si Brahim. The man she called the sheik was her husband, who had been arrested at the very beginning of the war and disappeared as quickly without any trace. She refused to believe he was dead, persevering in the hope of his return, and endlessly questioned people. Hassan shook his head no.

"What! People don't know the sheik in Algiers!" she resumed aggressively, fully determined to wheedle an affirmative reply out of the adolescent.

Hassan gave an embarrassed look around him. A young man

with a coarse accent intervened. "Be reasonable, auntie. How can you expect people to talk about the sheik in Algiers? The sheik met his death in our area. You've already been told that."

"Since he is dead, let's search for his remains."

She pulled her veil up over her legs as if she were preparing to undertake a long trek over roadways filled with pitfalls.

"Auntie, we don't know where Si Bachir was killed. There are so many ravines and grottoes. How do you expect us to find him? We'll search. We're already searching."

Visibly irritated at having to go over the same matter he had surely talked about dozens of times, the young man made an effort to soften his voice and to adopt a conciliatory tone in a way one tries to ward off a litany of grievances from people who aren't quite in their right minds.

The bones gathered up by Didou and Lahcen were placed on a sheet that Si Brahim's mother delicately folded and tied up with the help of the red-fringed green scarf. She was still crying and, despite the urging of various people, she would not taste either the warm cakes spread out on a raffia tray or the milk brought out in two pitchers by two young girls from Saïd's house. The old man did not eat anything either. He went on talking, and his son, who never stopped chewing, showed his agreement by nodding his head and grunting.

"I said, 'The rifle I don't give up.' 'Come on, Uncle Saïd, you know you've got a rifle with a fancy butt on it. People told us.' 'Yes, I had a rifle like that, but I sold it a long time ago.' I told the brothers: 'Why worry about a rifle, as old as I am!' God forgive me, children. I didn't want to give up the rifle. The *moudjahadin*, the warriors, were our children, they were fighting for us, but the rifle, the rifle was my soul. Can you give up your soul? So I dug a hole in my house at the same place where I say my prayers. I wrapped up the rifle and cartridges in wool cloth and leather, and I buried it all. . . . Now that peace has returned, children, I can say praise be to God! In this house, God and his saints are always revered. When the war started, my son Ali said, 'Father, let's leave this house and go live in the village. We'll find a house to rent. Here we're in danger.' I said, 'My son, we never have left our home or our garden or our fields. If it's our destiny to die in the home of our ancestors, let us accept it.' God and his saints protected us. The brothers came by at night and we gave them food. The French soldiers came by in daytime and found me in front of the door of the house. 'So, old man, you didn't see any jackals?' I answered, 'The jackals don't come this way,' and they left. Only one time did they enter the house. They searched thoroughly and then they left. . . . When peace returned, I got out the rifle, cleaned it, charged it, then I saddled the mare, the old mare over there, the one I call the white one. I hadn't ridden her in seven years' time. I said to myself: 'Saïd, Saïd, are you still able to put on the saddle? You who people called Saïd the Lightning Bolt because you used to be as fast as lightning.' No, I'm joking. I wasn't afraid of mounting the white mare. She was as old as I, but the rifle? Yes, I was frightened about the rifle. I said, 'Maybe it won't shoot any more, that rifle.' Seven years under the ground is a long time. . . . "

The gendarmes were the last French officials still present in the village, a total of a dozen men who only left their barracks to go shopping in the market, wearing no military insignia and without their former self-confidence. Before the referendum, one of them who was having trouble giving up his conventional behavior as representative of French order was insulted, or close to it, right in the street by an Algerian. The gendarme tried to tear off a wall the first poster recounting the history of the Algerian resistance movement.

"Don't touch that."

The man who had spoken, stressing every syllable to make it clear that this was a serious warning, was standing one meter from the gendarme, erect, a red tarboosh perched on his head, a long pipe in his hand. His eyes were hard and staring.

"These posters are against the law," said the gendarme in a voice tempered by surprise, his index finger pointing toward the wall as if to recover the force and legitimacy of the accusation.

"You have no orders to give us. Algeria is independent. Get the hell out!"

The man stepped forward. He was standing in front of the poster, tightfisted, the pipe between his teeth jutting out like a weapon. The gendarme stepped back, face contorted, and stammered something like, "That we'll see!" Then he walked off down the middle of the street, alone and unsteadily, under the mocking gaze of the onlookers who had gathered on both sidewalks.

The gendarmes passed the time of day on the steps of their barracks, standing there, silent, arms dangling. From time to time their wives appeared in the second-story window, would peer out anxiously and then disappear. Their children no longer went running through the garden—not since Algerian youngsters had thrown stones at them and called them obscene names. Upset by the changes that had come about in the lives of their parents and villagers, they remained seated on the steps with their playthings scattered around them. Sometimes they would get up and put their nose against the wire fence, inquisitive, pensive, and secretly tormented by the desire to be a part of the celebrations going on on the other side.

On the other side of the street, right across from the gendarmes, as if to thumb their nose at these holdover representatives of the deposed regime, the Independence celebrations went on at full swing the whole day long. On the tennis and *boules* courts, around the little refreshment stand whose shutters had been repainted green—where the French from the village used to hang out—the Algerians, freed from their anguish, repressing in the depths of silence memories they have stripped bare, were laughing, dancing, and sprinkling the sky with salvos to victory. They emptied bottles of lemonade as they gave thanks to God for having driven out the oppressors. Head high, they listened to patriotic marches chanted by the scouts, and with a touch of nostalgia for tradition, took up the refrains of sentimental ballads broadcast over loudspeakers hanging from the trees. They observed several minutes of silence in homage to the martyrs, sometimes troubled by the untimely coughing that stirred up a concert of reproving "*sh!*'s." They wildly applauded the vague speeches whose delirious accounts of heroism and words of promise sent them into raptures of enthusiasm.

In the evening, scouts performed plays in which collaborators and opportunists were taunted, manhandled, and strongly denounced. Accepted by everyone as a harmless adolescent game, these activities, previously unknown in the village, attracted a large crowd. The spectators, seated on the gravel—women and girls on one side, men and boys on the other—laughed as they had never laughed before. Often the action moved out into the audience. Spectators invented replies that they shouted at the actors, using the person's name or the character's name. Others, unhappy with the course of the action and replies, interrupted with calls for order and with threats. Everyone else laughed.

The most comic moments were provoked by the intervention of parents whose children were playing parts.

"Chaban! Thank you, my son! Thank you and a thousand times thanks! That is how you honor your father. You let people cover him with insults in full public view. Good-for-nothing!" a spectator called out to her son.

The latter, in the role of a collaborator, had just undergone humiliating treatment from his comrades, the revolutionaries, who had shaken him severely and called him "garbage" and "son of a bitch."

Another evening, people rolled on the ground holding their sides with laughter. Merbouha, an elderly country woman who had recently moved to the village, stood up in the middle of the audience, pale with anger, her emaciated arms stretched out toward the stage where a young colossus with gentle eyes lent himself docilely and delightedly to the most derisive roles.

"Hachemi! Why do you let them push you around? Defend yourself, idiot!"

Seated on a bench and holding himself erect, Hachemi was smiling with obvious pleasure. A young man wearing a white smock was concentrating on cutting Hachemi's hair with a noisy pair of clippers. Without a doubt, the barber was truly doing his job. Hair was falling in big tufts onto the impassive shoulders of his client. "Why are you letting yourself be shaved like a she-goat! Get down from there, you wretched child! God curse you!"

Unmoved, Hachemi allowed his head to be half shaved. When he finally left the stage, his mother slumped to the ground and burst into tears, surrounded by her neighbors who didn't know whether to comfort her or to make fun of her. Things didn't stop there. Shortly after that, the wretched child reappeared on stage, this time trotting on all fours and decked out with a pair of enormous donkey ears, a peasant with a happy face astride his back. Merbouha, numbed by her distress, took this like a slap in the face. She reacted like a watchspring let loose, standing, facing the stage, gesticulating, shouting, her voice filled with indignation and despair.

"Oh you wretch! Now you're changed into a donkey! May God change you into a monkey, for good! I swear by these mountains I'll break my cane on your back."

"Calm yourself, Merbouha. It's only a game. We're in the theater," ventured one spectator.

"Thee-ater or no thee-ater, I don't give a darn. That boy is covering me with ridicule and is making me the laughing stock of the earth."

Hachemi gave his mother the final blow by suddenly starting to bray and then pretending to let some thunderous farts. Merbouha dug her fingers into her cheeks, and the audience, dying of laughter, no longer knew whether the son or the mother was the better comedian of the two.

The occasions of collective circumcision, begun with Independence, also took place on the tennis courts. First organized in honor of the sons of soldiers who disappeared in combat, they were later opened to the poor families of the village. In their white robes, green scarf at the neck, the children came riding on the back of a grandmother, an older sister or in a relative's arms, some laughing, others suspicious, some crying softly, others screaming with fright. Seated cross-legged on mats, two musicians struggled for their flute and tambourine to be heard above the firing of hunting rifles and automatic weapons. The circumciser, sleeves pushed back, honeyed up to the children, gently took hold of the penis, exposed the gland, smoothed out the foreskin, and then told them to look at the big airplane up in the sky. When each child got over his surprise, the scissor-hands had already done their work. Blood. Then came endless howls of pain and despair against the trickery and deliberate treachery: hadn't they been told they were being taken to a celebration where they would be painlessly circumcised? People crowding around them encouraged their nascent sense of virility by ovations and risqué banter as family members dropped money into cupped green scarves.

The *harkis* had behaved in many different ways. Those who were deeply involved with the French had not hesitated to follow the French army, often leaving their families behind without any means of support. Moussa, paralyzed many years before by a bullet from the FLN, had left the village, people said, hidden in a wicker trunk. The French army had not waited for him. The clever *harkis* didn't take that much trouble. They were happy just to move to another village. With no one in their new location to give away their past, they slipped themselves into the newly born State, many taking over positions of responsibility. Those who did not feel that they had overly compromised themselves, who had regularly paid the revolutionary levy, and had furnished ammunition to the underground, looked the other way when there were suspects, or quite simply because they had never harmed anyone, had stayed on in the village, trying to go unnoticed, to be forgotten, avoiding at all costs showing themselves in public for fear of being taken to task by people who knew nothing except that they had worked side by side with the French.

Their families, on edge, kept a lookout, while the neighbors, either commiserating or ferocious, took pity on their bad luck or made fun of their concern.

"After all, we're not going to kill them and leave their children orphans. They've done no harm. The criminals have left for France."

"Ha! Ha! Yesterday they were parading in their French uniforms, and look at them today. Like a bunch of women. Locked up at home all day. All they need is a scarf and a dress."

Others, in order to escape the inferno of uncertainty, had turned themselves over to the military authorities, saying that they had never harmed anyone and that by staying at home they risked being carried off and killed. Their guards, jubilantly adopting the methods of yesterday's torturers, treated them with brutality and cynicism. The inmates were submissive, accepting every demeaning chore, conscious that in prison at least they were being protected.

The hunt for collaborators began at the end of August. The abductions were carried out at night by young men, last-minute militants who considered it their right to render justice, avenge the dead, and purify the land. They executed by revolver, knife, and hatchet in secret grottoes or distant ravines. The victims' relatives, without recourse or right to complain, suffered their distress in silence as they listened to rumors. And everything finally came out, what had happened taking shape in whispers in their atrocity, with persons' names, itineraries, stops, and details that left no ray of hope.

There were killings in the village. Tayeb was abducted one night as he left the café next to his house where, since he had left the French army, he spent the day and part of the night dressed in his Sunday best playing dominoes. The people of the neighborhood, who had known him for years, said nothing. One single time, a young boy who had formerly worked in a bistro where *harkis* came to get drunk spat on him before he ran off yelling, *"Harki*, you're a marked man!"* Witnesses to the scene acted as though they had heard and seen nothing. Tayeb did not try to chase the boy as any other adult insulted by a tenderfoot normally would have done. He wiped off the spittle stuck to his thigh, and he took on a faraway look. No doubt he was recalling the bistro when its windows were covered with wire mesh as protection against terrorist grenades, the bistro where after he had drowned his fears for tomorrow in beer, he stretched out his hand to caress the plump buttocks of the young waiter hounded at every turn by the desire to sodomize him.

The man who operated the movie had never worn a uniform, but he too was abducted. Hassan, like most of the children, did not like him because of his mania for passing through the auditorium without warning carrying a flashlight to ferret out freeloaders. The quick of mind who, as soon as the lights went down, had rushed back to the most comfortable and most expensive seats, got a resounding slap and were taken without further ado to the first row, a few inches from the screen. Adults didn't like him, either, since the day he had hurried to the police station, whether truly in a panic or moved by a desire for revenge, to make the declaration that he had just escaped from an ambush set up by two young *fellagas* on the road to Sétif. The two young *fellagas*, two adolescents armed with clubs, were buried the next day, a bullet hole in the chest.

On the other hand, there were those who were moved to pity over Chouchi's death. Before he became a *harki*, he had worked for Hassan's father, irrigating, weeding, and digging in the garden. At about eleven o'clock, Hassan would take him something to eat, some bread from the bakery, dates, and sometimes a package of cigarettes to be charged against his salary. His strong wrists were wrapped in wide straps of leather studded with copper.

"You see how strong I am."

He flexed his arms. His muscles swelled up like small mountains.

"Touch to see how hard. I can break down a wall."

Then one day Hassan ran into him in a soldier's uniform complete with blue forage cap and shoes that resounded on the pavement. He was big, handsome, strong. He offered Hassan four *douros*. And the child, who had always been afraid of soldiers, especially those accompanied by dogs, had the feeling that nothing could happen to him: Chouchi, his friend, was there to protect him. He would also protect his family and all his neighbors. And indeed when Hassan's father was arrested,

Chouchi interceded with the captain and brought about his release within a week.

One night there was a commotion in the yard of the neighbors that Chouchi's family shared with other families. Chouchi opened the gate wide. He was just about to go to his barracks as usual when he saw two silhouettes behind the trees. He stepped inside and locked the gate.

"They're there! They're going to kill me! I'll take care of them!"

He was shouting. His voice trembled. His wife, his mother, and his neighbors rushed out into the yard and surrounded him.

"I'll take care of them, I tell you!"

He pulled a grenade out of his pocket. Everybody grabbed his arms, begging him not to use it. His wife tearfully embraced him.

"If you throw a grenade, we will all be dead."

A week later, Chouchi moved into a house near the barracks where a number of *harkis* were already living. Shortly after that he completely disappeared from the village. He was not to come back until after the cease-fire, when he opened up a fruit and vegetable stall right across from the former barracks, now occupied by soldiers of independent Algeria: nostalgia, thoughtless provocation, a suicide wish, or chance?

However that may be, Chouchi was there, and the soldiers, in their comings and goings, saw him and knew he was there. They said nothing to him and bought nothing from him. He didn't look his clients squarely in the face for fear they might detect something suggestive in his eyes to his disadvantage, something that might bring on injury and humiliation. He held his head low, contracting his large body as much as he could. Then suddenly, as if lashed by a flash of pride and fury, he would straighten up, throw back his head in a moment of defiance and take a deep breath through his nostrils, with a look quivering with rock-hard energy. In instances of extreme tension, he seemed ready for any test. "Come on, if you want, and kill me! Yes, I was a *harki*, and everybody knew it!" He would go as far as the curbstone, working up a mouthful of spittle that he would spew violently into the gutter: a challenge to death or an attempt to empty his body of the anguish that filled it? A vain attempt, a vain hope. The next moment, fear was back again, coiled in his guts and twisting his body, holding him in a vise.

His wife prayed in silence, beseeching God not to make orphans of their children, these angels no bigger than a grain of ground wheat. She made him take the children to his stall. Her thinking, which she didn't dare express to him for fear of vexing him, was that the presence of the children at his side would guarantee a kind of moral immunity. Who would dare publicly to attack the father of a family surrounded by his children, innocent before both God and mankind?

The stranger hailed him by name. There was something of an order in the call, but the voice had a certain tone of reassurance, something almost familiar. He got up immediately, slipped on his espadrilles and went out without a backward glance. His wife and children, who had stopped eating, followed him with frightened, questioning eyes. Until then no one had ever called him at such an hour. He walked to the middle of the yard without haste or fear. His espadrilles clopped on the cement. His hand lifted the metal latch. The door grated open and, at the same moment, four hands grabbed hold of him, and without so much as the time to let out a cry or move to get away, he was already on the path that went behind the house, pulled, pushed, carried, and dragged along in a frantic flight in the direction of the mountain.

The hamlet's inhabitants were waiting on a threshing floor bordered with white millstones. As if for a celebration, there were men, women, and children. They encircled Chouchi. Cigarettes glowed. Rifle barrels gleamed under the moon. Chouchi was on his feet, slightly bent over, pallid in his white *gandoura*. His hands were trembling. His bare feet were bleeding. One man wrapped a long cord several times around his waist before knotting it in front like the kind of woolen belt worn by women. Another handed him a red scarf.

"Dance!"

And Chouchi, stiff and awkward, began to move.

"Wave the scarf!"

"Shake your ass!"

People guffawed. They clapped their hands. The women and children chanted together: "*Harki*, you're a marked man!"

"God send you the plague! You call that dancing?"

Chouchi, beyond any feelings of shame, danced as well as he could, made new attempts, twisted his body, streaming with sweat the whole time. No doubt he hoped that after this supreme humiliation, after he had made people laugh, he could leave alive. Then the shouting quieted down, and Chouchi stood immobile in the middle of the threshing floor, eyes haggard, mouth open, the red scarf hanging from his hand, his waist bound by a cord, his shadow crouching at his feet.

A strong authoritative voice broke the silence.

"Do you remember the things you've done?"

Chouchi's lips moved, but no sound came out.

"Let's hear from you, Amar."

"I remember everything. It was winter. They were on the road to the well over there. This guy had a machine gun, a big one. I already knew who he was. He began to curse and insult us. 'I'll mow you all down, to the last man! Ha! You think we don't know you've got *fellagas* at your houses every night! This is your last day. Say your prayers. . . . '"

Chouchi's lips didn't stop moving.

"And you, Aldja! Speak up!"

"He's the one. I recognize him. He cut open the semolina sacks. 'Have pity!' I said. 'Don't waste God's semolina. We are poor. You are a Muslim like us. Have pity on us!' And what did he do, the infidel, while I was crying? He emptied a box of red pepper on the semolina, then salt, and finally a container of gasoline. He started to laugh. 'Look, you've got the makings of a nice big cake for your children. . . . '"

"Why, my sister, why? I never did such a thing. I was never in your house."

"And old Hadj, it wasn't you who threw him into a ditch the day of the big police roundup? He wasn't walking fast enough."

"Why, brothers, why? I never pushed a man into a ditch."

"So, according to you, Uncle Hadj is a liar."

"Uncle Hadj, tell us what he did to you."

"Release him. If he did wrong, God will punish him."

"Uncle Hadj! He's surely the one who shoved you into the ditch the day of the police roundup! Did you forget?"

"The heart forgets nothing. Him or another, what difference? Release him. Let him go his way. Children, children, give the earth some rest. She has drunk so much blood. She has drunk so many tears!"

"Why, my brother, why? I've done nothing."

"Traitor!"

"Scoundrel!"

"Dog! You're the one who finished off Lamri. He tied him to the mule, showing no pity. Lamri said: 'Chouchi, my brother, you've known me for a long time, take it easy, don't tighten the cord. My chest's hurting.' He tightened the cord even more. Poor Lamri! Peace be with the souls of our martyrs. He died on arrival in the ambulance."

"I didn't do that. Why, brothers? I paid money to the underground, I had prisoners freed, I have four children. Nobody asked me to join the underground. If anybody'd asked me, I would have joined. I have children, four of them. . . ."

Chouchi was screaming. He was sobbing, slobbering, twisting in place, arms out in supplication. He beseeched everyone, men, women, and children. He swore by the flag with the red star, by the summer's harvest, by the high heavens, that he was innocent. At dawn three men dragged him away him by the cord, hands tied behind him, gagged with the red scarf. At the bottom of a ravine under a caper bush lay a shovel, a pickax, and a hatchet.

Sunday mornings were reserved for weddings. The processions were no longer formed, as in earlier times, of mules decked out in leather and furs, and little nervous horses mounted by solemn-looking men in white robes. They were no longer silent and stealthy as during the war. Since Independence, wedding processions only used automobiles: four or five for those not so well-to-do; twenty or more for those with money and who liked to do things up brown. While the small processions made do by marking their crossing of the village with a few honks of the horn, the important processions, flowing with flowers, bedecked with ribbons and flags, bristling with ill-tempered rifles, went from one end of the village to the other, the horn tooting the five notes of the Independence. People could tell what the bride looked like judging by the length of the line of cars and the intensity of the honking: either traditional, that is, the bride invisible under an opaque veil and surrounded by women, or—and this was the new custom—veiled, coiffed, and gloved in the French manner, bridegroom at her side. This new style gave rise to comments of indignation and despair.

"Is that what Independence is? Now we're marrying our girls in the nude. There's no more modesty. The French are gone, but we have inherited their shameless ways."

And so every Sunday there were tempestuous marriages, which also brought a harvest of legends, funny stories and, occasionally, dramas. You couldn't be sure any more on your wedding night of getting a virgin whose "acquisition" had just been celebrated. Independence had brought a lot of changes, effrontery and licentiousness. Rumors ran wild. One bridegroom, the night of his marriage, flew into a rage. His wife, calling on God and all his saints, swore that she was intact before he approached her, and his mother-in-law, who came running in outraged by the monstrousness of the accusation, yelled for all to hear that her daughter, pure as a *houri*, had never been face to face with a man in her whole life: so! The man, losing any sense of filial respect, had grabbed hold of his aged mother—she who had so highly praised the virtues of her future daughter-in-law—and had shaken her so violently that she fell to the ground with her veil off. She began to cry and then, shaking her fist at the sky, cursed her irreverent son for the rest of his days, before falling into a stony silence. The groom had publicly called his in-laws garbage and, deaf to all reason, accompanied his wife back to her parents' home the next morning.

. . .

Families paid no attention to the cost of celebrating a marriage or a circumcision. The poor took out loans in order to show off, and the rich profited from the occasion to display their wealth. Great feasts were organized. Guests were no longer received in well-to-do households as before. They were separated according to fortune and position. Important guests had the right to a chair, a table, an individual place setting, and to a serving that included, in addition to the traditional couscous, vermicelli soup, ratatouille of green peppers and tomatoes, lemonade, little cakes, and an assortment of fruits. As for the others, the majority, invited as a courtesy or needed to flatter the host's vanity, they all ate from the same platter of couscous and drank from the same water pitcher, seated cross-legged on mats.

The women gathered by themselves, happy after so many years of silence to be able to sing and dance within the limitations authorized by the men. In the street outside the house, men and boys circled around the musicians. Rich people sent to Sétif for dancers dressed in transparent robes, wearing heavy jewelry and perfume. They swayed from side to side waving scarves that now and then they threw over a male shoulder as a sign of seduction. Eloquent fingers slipped banknotes between their breasts. They laughed and expressed thanks with an amorous look and a special twist of the hips. Winks, sighs, and expressions of desire were exchanged. After the dancers left, the young men got together to rent a taxi and went off to find the girls in the big city. Unable to stifle their desires, they would go straight to a brothel—minors sneaking in or buying their way past the man at the door—and there, in the darkness of a cubicle with whitewashed walls, on a mat covered with a cold sheet, they experienced the burning sensation of a precocious ejaculation. After that, their heads filled with new images of voluptuousness, they would go to a bar to consume as much forbidden alcohol as they could. At midnight they staggered home, pockets empty but their senses appeased, making as little noise as possible so as not to awaken the father.

In the month of September, huge trucks, chartered by the commune, brought tons of wheat and margarine to the village—a contribution, supposedly, from the Americans. People provided with sacks and straw baskets came from everywhere and lined up the length of the hangar where the distribution was to take place. People called down praise and benedictions on the new leaders of their country, their brothers in Islam who were so responsive to their misery. They waited patiently, but their disappointment was great: a large part of the manna had disappeared as if by enchantment, so the ration given to each family was quite small, a few pounds of grain and a container of margarine. The frustration of the beneficiaries was even greater when they got home and found that the American wheat was black and hardened, and the big tin-plate containers did not contain real butter. The wheat was given to the chickens, and the cans of margarine, emptied of their contents, were made into buckets.

Young people and the unemployed lived in a feverish daydream. Newspaper and radio announcements, repeated and embellished from mouth to ear, plus the proclamations of local officials, promised everybody a radiant future of work and self-realization. The People's State generously gave her sons the most desirable posts and professions: schoolteacher, reporter, pilot, technician, administrative official, policeman, and director of farms and of factories. People who had never been to school could become mechanics, drivers of farm machines, health agents, soldiers or gendarmes if they had the required height and weight. For those who no longer could be educated, modern factories and gigantic industries were being opened up. These promises attracted large numbers of villagers working in France and incited many a peasant to leave home and fields behind. The possibility of an urban existence and a fixed salary won out over any other reasonable consideration.

Mabrouk, Hassan's cousin, wanted to become a policeman. Since the day he had filed his candidacy, responding favorably to the requirements for weight and height, he no longer wanted to accompany his father to the forest. Going to fetch wood on the back of a she-ass seemed to him unworthy of his future status as a representative of the law. In the morning, by dint of flattery and promises, he would talk his mother out of a few coins and stroll through the village, an old transistor slung over his shoulder. In the afternoon he would choose a table at the back of the café and play dominoes with other young men, future aviators or future policemen like himself.

Lahcen, Hassan's brother, freed from the local militia, wanted to get into the gendarmes. As a former soldier, he thought his candidacy would present no problems. He was wrong. He was two centimeters short of the required height: Algeria did not want a corps of gendarmes made up of midgets. Lahcen spat behind himself as he left the recruiting office. He did not look for other work. A week later, he embarked once more for France. A friend of his father had advanced him the travel money.

The march left from the stadium, led by two young employees of the agricultural organization and a group of boyscouts brandishing placards and flags. At night they had covered facades with big red letters calling for a massive mobilization against the survivors of the colonial regime who were still in top administrative posts, for example, in that agricultural association. The collaborators were designated by name and people were asked to run them out. "Aboudi to the firing squad! Down with Aboudi!" they yelled in French.

In all this collective spirit of peacetime, Hassan could not recapture the enthusiasm and jubilation of former days when, at school, the students had refused to go back to class or to eat to show their solidarity with a student who had been expelled or when men and women, side by side in the street, chanted their feelings of revolt and despair. Great numbers of young people, delighted to make noise with impunity right in town, gave resounding kicks to the storekeepers' garbage pails, crushed cartons and empty cans strewn in the gutters, ran from one side of the sidewalk to another dodging around people's legs, made the public fountains spray, invented obscene slogans, and responded with sneers to dirty looks from their elders. Some people did not hide their satisfaction, glad that finally there was a public attack—even if only verbally from the mouths of adolescents—against those who built their power on collaboration with the colonial administration and who seemingly were unmoved by anything. Other people seemed vaguely upset. How could kids be allowed to boo and drag through the mud a family as respectable as the Aboudis who had given the region illustrious leaders for more than a century and who possessed so many wheat fields, autos, and friends among the new authorities.

Near the drinking trough, the demonstrators ran right into one of the Aboudi sons in his car. They encircled the auto, kicking and hitting the frame, and spitting on the windows and windshield. The motor roared, and the auto easily broke through the menacing crowd. The demonstration quieted down beside the drinking trough as quickly as it had begun in the stadium. It had lasted no more than an hour, but it was not without results: in the following weeks the Aboudi family left the village and went to settle elsewhere, in other towns where they lacked neither the goods nor the friendships with which to continue a life of comfort.

"Mama, enough of charlatans! I don't want to hear any more about those thieves. They'll cram my eyes so full of filth I'll end up blind."

"God bless you, son. Let me have my heart's desire. As long as my legs can hold me, I'll walk, I'll go everywhere. They say people come so far to see him, and that he cures the crazy, the sick who never walked, and women who never conceived. God bless you, don't stand in my way! Let me run till I die. When I see boys your age with their eyes open like windows and I think about you, my soul half melts. All the women are happy except for me. . . . "

Fatim-Zohra began to cry as she did every time she talked about her son's illness, and Hassan, torn to shreds by those tears, said not a word. Fatim-Zohra easily found several women neighbors as desirous as she to consult the new healer who had performed so many miracles that they still did not know about. They hired a taxi and left early with baskets and scarves filled with gifts.

The healer who simultaneously fulfilled the functions of sage and diviner didn't look anything like his already established colleagues. He was young, had a rosy complexion, wore a beret, a short-sleeved shirt, a wristwatch, straight trousers, and black moccasins. A massive wooden coffer placed in front of a woolen blanket stretched on a cord to resemble a curtain served him as a seat during his consultations. People said he was the spouse of a female *djinn* he had met in France while working in a hospital where he did the cleaning, took food to the patients, and pushed the patients' carts. The wife had appeared to him at the end of a deserted corridor wearing a white doctor's outfit the night of the Mouloud festival. She had taken him by the arm.

"Fear nothing, brother. I am a Muslim *djinn*. There is no God but Allah, and Mohammed is His Prophet. My name is Fatima. I shall marry you, and we will go home. Algeria will soon be independent. Let us care for the believers."

After listening to the complaints and prayers of the patients, he withdrew behind the woolen blanket to confer with Fatima, visible only to him, about the therapy to propose to the sick. Voices—now serious, now sharp—stifled laughter, sighs, and the rustling of a dress could be heard.

Inspired by Fatima, whose business sense seemed very sharp, the young sheik transformed a part of his house into an ultramodern clinic. A veritable treatment center, naturally all invisible, was set up. There were offices to issue appointments, X rays for photographing the inside of the body, injections and operations carried out without pain by the omnipresent and omnicompetent Fatima. The sick, aged persons who were semi-invalids were left there by their families to be cared for in exchange for a gift in kind or money; they were bedded down side by side on thatched mats, fed on little cakes and couscous with milk, and received a blessing every morning from the mouth of the youthful sage.

When Fatim-Zohra's turn came, the sheik, after having consulted Fatima behind the curtain, declared, "Next Saturday, we will come to examine Monsieur Hassan, son of Fatim-Zohra and of Youssef, age fifteen, who has been struck in the eyes by infidel *djinns*."

On the expected day, the healer did not appear. He presented himself a week later in the late afternoon.

"Excuse me. If we did not come last Saturday, it is because the dossier of Monsieur Hassan had not arrived at the office. Without files, we can do nothing."

Youssef went off with a nervous cough, and Hassan, who in his mind could envision his files being delivered by angels or demons through the corridors of the sky, almost burst into laughter. Fatim-Zohra devoutly kissed the plump hands of her guest, one of God's blessed. The sheik asked for a bowl of oil and a spoon, and closed himself in a room with his patient.

"Stand up, and unbutton your shirt. Fatima is going to take an X ray of you."

Hassan, half perplexed, half amused, asked why an X ray of the thorax, then said to himself, "After all, why not?" He had had a lot of X rays at the hospital. That's really how to proceed to find out the cause of an illness. Fatima knows what she must do. He bared his chest and remained standing in the middle of the room, embarrassed by his hands he had decided not to put in his pockets. Maybe he would have to stretch out his arms in front of him, a bit apart, like clasping the X ray machine at the hospital.

Chest bare and elbows finally bent to a halfway position like some long-distance runner, Hassan patiently waited five minutes, ten minutes, a quarter of an hour, a half hour, then began to find that Fatima worked decidedly too slowly. No doubt she liked work carefully done. He moved his weight from leg to the other several times, audibly sighed, and discreetly cleared his throat. Nothing worked. The healer, withdrawn into a corner, seemed to have forgotten he was there. Hassan coughed still more loudly, let out a grunt, called himself an imbecile, and went over to sit down on the bed as he straightened out his clothing. The healer stirred the spoon in the bowl of oil for some time before calling Fatim-Zohra.

"The results are there. Fatima has just brought back the X rays. Look carefully."

He showed her the bowl full of oil. Fatim-Zohra attentively leaned over.

"Tell me what you see."

"I don't know, Master," answered Fatim-Zohra timidly.

"Look carefully, here in front of you. You surely see a crescent."

He was silent for a moment.

"It certainly is a crescent. How is it formed?"

Fatim-Zohra, feeling embarrassed and guilty at seeing nothing lowered her head to the floor.

"Tell me, what is its shape? This crescent is open."

"Perhaps, Master."

"What do you mean, perhaps? This crescent is open. There's no doubt about it."

"I can't make it out very clearly, Master."

"Well I can. I see it. It's clearly there in the oil, well outlined, open, but not too much so. The day that the two horns touch, your son will recover his sight. And that day, you can believe me, is not far off."

The young sheik had Fatim-Zohra sit down in front of him and told her in detail what treatment to follow to hasten Hassan's recovery. First there would be nineteen intramuscular injections administered by Fatima. She would carry out her operations during the night while Hassan was asleep, without pain. This would be followed by taking the oil in the bowl to massage the sick boy's chest nineteen evenings at a stretch. And then there were prescriptions to be observed: eat no salt for nineteen days, not leave the house for nineteen days, and not wash his body for nineteen days.

The healer asked twenty-five thousand—sufficient to maintain a whole family comfortably for a month. Youssef, who was trying to keep himself from throttling the charlatan, did not argue: he handed him five thousand and unceremoniously sent him on his way. He turned his anger against his wife.

"It is a sin to believe what those robbers tell you. How could such scoundrels be part of God's designs?"

"Hold your tongue, man! We are doing this for our son. Don't ruin the effects of the treatment with your complaining. God has said, 'Try, oh my creature! And I shall help you reach your goal.'"

Fatim-Zohra believed so completely in the word of the young sheik that that night—the first night when the invisible Fatima was to perform her healing—stretched out beside her son to watch over his sleep, she got up with a slight limp. She asked her son if he had felt something in his sleep, something like an injection in the buttock, for example.

"No, I didn't feel anything," replied Hassan, who burst out laughing.

"Well, my son, I did feel something. I've got a pain in the buttock, as though someone had given me an injection during the night. I didn't have any trouble at all yesterday."

"It's clear, Mama, that Fatima mistook her patient. She gave you the shot instead of me."

Fatim-Zohra's buttock hurt her all day long, and she was certain that she had been given a shot by the *djinn*, who, be it said, must not have had a very gentle hand.

If the father refused to listen to talk about spirits and remedies related to magic, he did believe in traditional medicines called Arabic, based on ores, roots, extracts of vegetables, animal fats, and other substances, which could be purchased in the market, the *souk*, or prepared at home from recipes transmitted by a trustworthy person. One day, one of the customers, certainly well-intentioned, advised Youssef to take a pigeon, cut its throat, clean it well, and then bind it with strips of cloth, opened out, over the eyes of the patient for three days and three nights: it was a remedy that had been tried by hundreds of persons since time immemorial and whose effectiveness was never in doubt. Hassan put up with the nauseating mask of sticky flesh for one day and one night.

161

One day, advised by a friend no less charitable than the other, Youssef brought home an old countryman who was a past master in the art of bleeding. After the usual preparations—the nape of the neck shaved with scissor and razor—Hassan got down on all fours, his head over an empty basin. He was hardly reassured: the hands of the old man were trembling slightly. Cuppings, propitiatory formulas, incisions with a Gillette blade. The blood spurted out, thick, abundant, hot on the neck, brushing against the corners of the lips, and trickling down the chin. Hassan had a sudden start. Nausea grabbed him in the throat. He thought of the lamb at the Aïd festival, throat cut so ineptly it was able to get to its feet again, frightened and shaking with spasms. Fatim-Zohra, upset by the sight of the blood, ran out into the courtyard. Youssef watched in silence. The countryman seemed pleased with his operation.

"Just look at that blood as black as soot! The humors of evil are flowing! You're going to have a body cleansed and your eyes washed and as limpid as the spring at Guergour, my child!"

The little vision that was still left to him held out until the October day when his father brought a rod of copper sulfate from the *souk*. Hassan rebelled, but then he gave in to the entreaties of his mother, who begged him to try to see just one more time, and so he passed the rod between his eyelids for a long time, meticulously, as if to provoke the irreparable, to get out of the fog that he had lived in for nine months, to go fully into darkness since getting well had proved impossible. The effect was overwhelming: Hassan's eyes began to flow like fountains, and, bit by bit, a vast night traversed by a serpent of turquoise that seemed to unite heaven and earth, a serpent that danced, alighted on his eyelids. As the days went by, blackness absorbed the blue and green serpent and unloosed innumerable elusive points of light.